The Elder Chronicles
Volume 2

Birth of a Savior

By

Robyn Kelly

This story is fiction. The settings are imaginary. Any resemblance of the characters or places to actual persons or places is purely coincidental.

© 2015, Robyn Kelly
Box 266
Howey in the Hills, Fl
TheElderChronicles@yahoo.com

Table of Contents

Prologue

The Elders were an ancient people. They had lived in peace for many thousands of generations on a small planet orbiting a star in a galaxy many light years from Earth. They maintained a vast storehouse of knowledge and often acted as mediators in disputes between other planets. They also ran an interstellar, and occasionally intergalactic, transport business. They were a well-known and respected race.

Very recently in the overall scheme of things, the Elder planet, which they referred to as Elderhome, was attacked by a fierce and powerful race in search of food and slaves. Having established no defense against such an attack, the Elders were forced to flee Elderhome.

A small band of Elders, quite by accident, landed on the Earth at approximately 1000 CE, local time, in the area now known as Arizona. They were ill equipped to survive on their own and would have indeed perished, but for help from a totally unforeseen source. Eventually, they made a home for themselves in a large butte, the center of which had collapsed long ago.

Any humans who might have witnessed the arrival of the Elders left no record of having done so. As time passed the United States Government created a reservation for a small Indian tribe in the immediate area of the Elders' home.

The tribal Shaman, for reasons of his own, declared that the area around the butte was sacred ground. He built a cabin in a small canyon at the southern end of the butte. To ensure their future safety, the Elders eventually revealed their existence to the Shaman and asked for his protection. Over time the Shaman, and his successors, became the Elders' only contact with the outside world.

To the other members of the tribe, the Elders melted into ancient lore and mythology. Modern day members of the tribe, if they thought of the Elders at all, relegated them to fanciful stories told to children.

Now, as our story continues, we look in on the Elder community as it exists in the 1980's.

Chapter 1

Wanderlust

Lisa was lying on her back, on the top edge of the butte, looking up at the stars. It was a clear night and the view was spectacular. Somewhere out there, she thought, among all those millions of stars and galaxies was Elderhome. She thrilled to think that she might even be able to see its sun. "Highly unlikely," she thought, "but what if?"

She loved to imagine what it might be like to be there instead of here. Lisa was a romantic. She was also on guard duty.

Whenever Lisa was assigned guard duty, she would gladly climb the steep path to the top of the butte. There she would spend her time looking out at the world around the butte. During the day there was the vast expanse of the Arizona desert to the west with mesquite trees, scrub brush and the occasional blooming cactus. There were the mountains to the north, easily visible on a clear day. On the eastern side was the Indian town of Wakulla, barely visible, except for the two-story hotel, which housed a small casino and was brightly lit at night. During the night there were the stars. Especially on clear nights, Lisa would just lie on her back staring out into the vastness of space.

If she tired of looking at the outside world, Lisa could just as easily roll over and observe whatever was happening inside the butte. The north end contained a thick growth of pine trees broken up by the two low domes that marked the sleeping quarters and the long dome that covered the supply bunker. To the south, the trees thinned out and the Council chambers were visible.

All day and all night at least two Elders were posted on the top of the rock walls that enclosed the butte. They were supposed to watch for any intrusion by planes, vehicles, hikers or rock climbers. Lisa had never seen anyone wandering around the scared ground. She had heard about a couple of rock climbers a few years ago.

Apparently the Shaman, Grey Wolf, and the reservation sheriff, Johnny Eagle, had sent them running in fear for their lives. They never returned and no one else has ever tried to repeat their effort.

As these and other thoughts popped up in Lisa's mind they were briefly considered and then dispatched. Sometimes Lisa just wondered what would become of her; what would her life be like. Lisa had never been a typical Elder. A true Elder would just do what she was told without always questioning the value of it. Neither was Lisa a true rebel; but she yearned for something the others did not need: excitement, adventure, fun. None of that was readily available in the Elder community. At least not in the quantity that Lisa wanted.

Lisa did her best to be a good Elder. She did what was asked of her without overt complaint and she tried to keep her lust for adventure under control. She knew that her chances of ever getting out of the butte that housed the Elder community were slim to none. She also knew that, should she ever get out into the world of humans, there would be great danger, even life-threatening danger. The butte had offered the Elders safety for a thousand years. Why risk such a good thing? And yet ...

When Lisa wasn't working or eating or sleeping, she often spent time in the supply bunker. That bunker was located in the center of the butte and contained all of the equipment, articles, clothing and artifacts that the Elders had amassed over their tenure on Earth.

Lisa was primarily interested in the books and maps. As she studied the maps she imagined the land they described: the mountains and rivers, the forests and towns. Occasionally, she would come across maps that covered the same area at different dates. She would then marvel at the changes that time wrought. Unfortunately, Lisa had no understanding of scale. She had no comprehension of just how much territory Arizona encompassed, let alone the entire United States or the whole planet.

The books Lisa read fueled her passion for romance. They also gave her quite a misconception of what humans were really like. None of the books included a discussion of humans' passion for discrimination and the associated brutality. If they had, Lisa might have reconsidered her desire to travel among them.

Lisa's best friend among the Elders was Nela. The two had grown up together as children. Now that they were both adults, the friendship had grown into something more serious. Neither really wished to pair off and have children, still there was some strange attraction between them.

Lisa and Nela did spend a lot of their spare time together. Lisa regaled Nela with tales of excitement and adventure gleaned from the various books available in the supply bunker. She even invented new stories. This was great fun, but tales of excitement were not nearly as satisfying as the real thing would be. Or so Lisa thought.

Nela was a much more typical Elder. She was tasked with maintaining the Council chambers. She had many opportunities to observe the Council in session and even to overhear private discussions among the councilors. Most of these she properly kept to herself. But, every so often, when she and Lisa were lounging in the shade of the tall pine trees, she would pass on a tidbit or two from the Council.

"A few days ago," Nela whispered, "I heard two councilors talking about a couple being allowed to emigrate. Have you ever heard of 'emigrating'?"

Lisa thought for a few seconds, scrunching her nose to assist the process. "I don't think so," she finally replied. "What's it all about?"

Nela beamed for she was glad to be the source of new information. "From what I gathered, it means that a couple are allowed to leave the butte and establish a new colony somewhere else."

"Among the humans?" Lisa was at once fascinated and horrified.

"I guess so," came the response between bites of fungus. "They were talking about the procedure, so I it must be something that has happened before."

Lisa's mind was already running on overload. This could be the answer to all her dreams. To leave the butte and live among the humans ... To start a new colony – as the leader ... There would be danger, but there would also be adventure and excitement and honor. "Can you find out more?" Lisa's excited tone even surprised Nela.

"I'll try," said Nela, trying to be just a bit discouraging. "But it may take some time. I will have to wait for the right moment to ask."

And it did take time. Nela had to wait many days for the proper moment, and the proper person, to ask. In the meantime, she and Lisa also had to compose a story to explain how she knew about emigrating. They were certain that it wasn't common knowledge among the other Elders.

Nela finally decided it would be best to ask Ari-Alma. She was the newest, and youngest, of the councilors and seemed to have a pleasant personality. She was also not so jaded as some of those who were long-time Council members. Then Lena had to wait for a time when Ari-Alma was alone and not otherwise occupied.

Patience was not Lisa's long suit. Every time she saw Nela, she asked how things were going. Nela began to regret she had ever brought up the topic. It was only their long friendship and Nela's understanding of Lisa's temperament that made the impatience tolerable. Nela had to caution Lisa against going to the Council herself. Lisa would never be able to explain how she had heard about emigrating without getting both of them in trouble. Lisa reluctantly accepted that argument, but she was getting more impatient all the time.

Then, one day, the opportunity came. The Council had adjourned. Every one had left the chambers save for Ari-Alma who was collecting leftover notes from the podiums as Nela tidied up the audience area. When Ari-Alma left the dais, Nela approached her, bowed deeply and spoke in a quiet voice. "Ari-Alma, may I ask you a question?"

"Certainly," Ari-Alma replied pleasantly.

Nela had practiced many times for this moment, but the words came out haltingly and with some trepidation. "I have heard of 'emigrating', but I don't understand the term. Can you explain it?"

Ari-Alma hesitated for a moment, as though weighing what to say. "To emigrate," she answered, "means that two or more elders leave this butte to establish a new colony elsewhere. The Council does not usually allow elders to emigrate unless the population of the butte is high enough to demand it. What prompted your interest?"

Now it was Nela's turn to be careful. "I heard the word used and could not define it." She hesitated a bit too long before asking, "Is anyone emigrating at this time?"

Ari-Alma had just the faintest smile. "Are you thinking about emigrating?"

"Oh, no!" The response was too quick and Nela knew it.

Ari-Alma's smile broadened. "Well, just in case someone you know is, the procedure isn't too complicated. First, you have to develop a good solid plan and submit it to the Council. You need to specify where you will go, what you will do when you get there, how you intend to earn enough money to live on – you will not be able to grow enough fungus to sustain you for at least a year – and how you intend to establish and maintain a new colony."

Nela was looking somewhat daunted at all of this. It was obvious to Ari-Alma that emigrating was not Nela's idea. Still, just in case, she added kindly, "I will be happy to accept a plan and present it to the Council, when anyone is ready."

"Thank you, Ari-Alma," Nela stuttered, bowed quickly and fled from the Council chamber.

Nela knew that she would find Lisa on the west rim of the butte that night. She had a quick bite of fungus for supper and walked somewhat nervously up the narrow path to the top of the butte. As expected, Lisa was lounging beside a large boulder watching the darkening sky. A storm was forming. It would likely be a wet night.

10

"Hi," Nela called out as she approached. "I think I have the answer to emigrating."

That brought Lisa to life. She sprang up, dislodging some small stones that went clattering over the edge. "Tell me!" she pleaded.

Nela sat down carefully and explained what Ari-Alma had said. Develop a plan explaining where, what, how. She would take the completed plan to Ari-Alma. Then she mentioned the deal killer. "Ari-Alma didn't say so exactly, but she gave me the distinct impression that only couples would be allowed to emigrate."

Lisa sat down dejectedly. She wasn't a 'couple'. She hadn't even thought about pairing up with anyone.

Nela wasn't through. "There's something else. The Council will only permit anyone to emigrate when there are too many Elders in the butte. I don't know how many are too many. But the number in the butte drops every time a couple emigrates. If they are letting couples emigrate now, I have no idea how many more will be eligible before the number drops below the limit.?"

"You really are Little Miss Sunshine, aren't you?" Lisa complained.

"If you really want to emigrate, it looks like you have your work cut out for you," Nela offered apologetically. "Well, I guess I had better go now," she said, rising slowly to her feet. She was in no hurry, but could see no reason to remain. It was getting late and she had a full schedule the next day. Still, she lingered a moment more, just watching the wheels go around in Lisa's mind. Finally, Nela shrugged resignedly; Lisa was too wrapped up in thought to pay any attention to her. She gave up and wandered off to get some sleep.

It was two days later before Lisa again saw Nela. The latter was sitting under a pine tree after her chores, nibbling on some fungus. Lisa sat down on the ground beneath the tree where Nela was eating.

"Want some fungus?" Nela asked, offering Lisa a piece.

Lisa accepted the food and munched on it quietly.

"You said it, you know," Lisa said softly. "Only couples are allowed to emigrate. If I am to emigrate, it will have to be as part of a couple ..." The comment just trailed off.

Nela remained still, concentrating on her food. The seconds grew into an eternity. At last, she looked over at Lisa.

"Oh, piff!" Lisa exclaimed. "It's high time I grew up and stopped being such a twit. Nela, will you pair with me?"

"Just so you can emigrate?" The question came out quietly, with no recrimination. But it hung in the air, waiting.

"No, of course not!" Lisa raised up until she was kneeling directly in front of Nela. "We have been friends forever!", she exclaimed. Then she continued quietly, "Emigrate or no, I cannot think of anyone I would rather pair with. Dear Nela, *will* you pair with me?"

Nela's answer was simple, "Yes," she whispered.

Nela and Lisa slowly merged together, clutching each other. They remained there under the tree for a long time as the sun slowly set behind the butte.

Chapter 2

Making a Plan

The first item in the order of business for Lisa and Nela was a pairing announcement. And, being Elders, that had to be accompanied by a party. Lisa appropriated an old record player and records from the supply bunker. Nela discovered some soda pop and dried meat left over from another recent party. They found a nice spot near the Council chambers and announced the party. Then they got out of the way. Over one hundred Elders, almost everyone not on duty, came out to help the new pair celebrate. Even Ari-Alma came, representing the Council. There was much singing and dancing, and the celebration lasted for many hours. The next morning, when it was all over, Lisa and Nela spent several more hours cleaning up.

Then, since they were now officially a couple, Lisa and Nela had to move their meager belongings out of the bunker that housed the children and singles and find a space in the bunker designated for couples. Then it was back to work as though nothing had happened. But now in their spare time, Lisa and Nela had a clear objective: to develop a plan for emigrating.

When the two went over to the supply bunker to return the left-over party supplies, they started hunting for information. The supply bunker was a large, deep cave-like bunker in the middle of the butte, just north of the Council chambers. In it for a thousand years the Elders had stowed away everything they had ever found useful. Tools, clothes, appliances, much junk, which might some day be useful for something. The supply bunker also served as the Elders' vault. Cash money, coin, gold and silver ingots, jewelry, loose gems, anything they had ever used as a medium of exchange. It now lay here, unguarded, just waiting for a need to arise. No one knew the exact value; it had never been inventoried. Some of it, such as the Confederate money, was of no value. Other items were worth far more as collectibles than for their intrinsic value. But, to the Elders, the items had only such value as the service they might render.

The first decision Lisa and Nela had to make with regard to emigrating was where to go. They wanted to pick a spot that had a favorable climate. Elders were not overly concerned with climate; they had the ability to regulate their internal thermostats within some limits. Antarctica was definitely off limits. So was the Sahara. There had to be ample water and a cool climate to facilitate growth of the fungus. There had to be sufficient space to preclude direct human contact. And there also had to be space to grow the colony beyond the first couple of years. That meant that any large city or populated area was off limits. They also presumed that the Council wouldn't want the various colonies grouped too closely together.

Lisa knew the location of an atlas and some old maps she had previously studied. Nela looked for information on the climate data and Lisa searched for an out-of-the-way spot. They both studied the maps that were available. But maps alone don't tell the whole story. Lisa and Nela had to delve deeply into their racial memories to fill in some of the missing information. The farther toward a pole and the higher in elevation a place was, the colder it would likely be. The lower in elevation and the nearer the equator, the warmer. Where the butte was located, in the Arizona desert, it was hot and dry. They decided to stay in the same general latitude.

They also presumed that travel to their new colony should be relatively simple. Neither Lisa nor Nela had any experience with air or sea travel, and they considered these to be impractical. The less they had to associate with humans on the journey, the better. They also deemed a slower mode of travel to be more desirable. Somewhere they had heard that humans wanted to do everything in a hurry.

At last, Nela placed her finger on a map near the butte's location in Arizona and moved it deliberately toward the east. She struggled to move it in a straight line until she came to some low-lying mountains. "Here?" she asked.

Lisa looked at where Nela's finger had come to rest. "Ar-kan-sas?" she read the name on the map. "Okay", she said. "let's see what we can find out about 'Arkansas'."

The two started searching through the contents of the bunker, looking for anything that might describe Arkansas. They found – nothing. As they were about to give up, Nela turned up a pile of old books buried deep in the back of the bunker. Apparently, they hadn't been used in years, if ever. One of the books had a large 'A' printed on the cover. Nela opened it and found article after article on subjects beginning with the letter 'A'. Among the articles was a three-page entry on Arkansas.

From that article Rita and Nela learned that southwestern Arkansas was hilly and had many farms. Cattle, chickens and some crops were raised there.

"Bingo!" cried Lisa. "That's it. We can start a farm. Maybe raise chickens and some smaller animals. We'll have plenty of room to grow our colony and will have our own source of food until the fungus grows out.

"Somehow, I don't think it's going to be that easy," Nela interrupted Lisa's fantasy. "We don't know anything about raising animals."

"We can learn," Lisa suggested. "Anyway, it's the start of a plan."

Then there had to be some way for Lisa and Nela to earn money. Not a lot of money would be required, but a steady trickle. Winning the lottery was not a good option. Neither of the two Elders had any experience in that line. Guard duty and toilet maintenance didn't count for much. No one living in the butte was ever paid for anything. Neither, of course, did they have to pay for anything. Lisa and Nela realized it would not be that way in the human world.

Nela pointed out that some of the area in Arkansas included forests. Tree topping might be an option; but not if they were to work among humans. Almost every time an Elder left the butte, she dressed as a female human. Lisa agreed that there probably were not very many female human loggers.

"But maybe we can sell some eggs and milk for a source of money," Lisa persisted.

"Milk comes from cows," Nela pointed out. "Cows cost a lot of money to purchase and even more to feed. They also require a large barn, milking machines …"

"What about goats?" Lisa offered. "They are smaller, cheaper and can be milked by hand."

Nela thought a little more about that option. "Yum!" she said, "Fresh goat milk!"

"And Cheese!" added Lisa.

So it was agreed. They would become lady goat and chicken farmers in Arkansas.

The hardest question had been resolved. Now all that was left to do was to fill in the details. Lisa and Nela looked at each other. All that was left was quite a lot. They had no idea how to acquire the land. They should at least include a few possibilities in their petition. They started rummaging through the supply bunker. Nothing. Of course not; anyone who had emigrated would have taken that information with them.

There was only one way to get that information, and all the other data they needed. They would have to leave the butte.

Nela protested, "No way! I am not sneaking out of the butte! If we get caught, we will both be cleaning toilets for a year and will never be allowed to emigrate."

"All right," Lisa groaned, "I'll go. Let's make a list of what we need."

"Where are you going to go?" Nela protested. "There are no towns nearby and we have no transportation."

That stopped Lisa, momentarily. "Isn't the Shaman supposed to support us?" she asked. "I'll ask him to get us the answers we need."

"You wouldn't dare!" Nela exclaimed. "If the Council ever found out, we'd be cleaning toilets for the rest of our lives."

"Not 'us', just me," Lisa offered in way of sacrifice.

"But we're a couple!" Nela insisted. "Wherever you go, I go, too. Besides, how do you know he would even consider your request?"

"Logic," Lisa stated. "He's supposed to help us and we need help. Now let's make out that list."

For the rest of the day they racked their brains to create a complete list of their needs. Bus fare to ... where? Little Rock. Cost of farm ... 2-3 acres ... with house, barn? Yes. Livestock? One male goat, 3-4 females. Chickens? Yes, they would have fresh eggs and meat. Living expenses? Cost of living data. Eventually they had a list that looked pretty good.

Lisa and Nela patted themselves on the back and went out for food and drink. Later, after it had grown dark, Lisa took the list and headed for the south end of the butte.

"Are you sure you want to do this?" Nela asked as she walked alongside Lisa. She was still not in favor of this approach.

"No, I'm not," Lisa answered. "But do you know any other way to get the information?"

"Maybe we could ask the Council..." Lisa half-heartedly suggested.

"Nela!" Lisa was nervous enough as it was and Nela was not helping. " the Council is not there to run our errands for us. They are looking for a completed proposal. This is the only way I can think of. I don't like it; just give me a real alternative."

Nela just walked along, very afraid, with a helpless expression on her face.

Lisa gathered her courage as she quietly passed by the Council chambers. Nela followed meekly, still trying to think of some sort of an alternative.

The trees on the southern end of the butte had been used for a special building project many years ago, leaving the ground clear, except for a few leftover stumps. In the south wall of the butte was a small cave, which led, via a circuitous path, through the wall to a small canyon. In the canyon were a rustic log cabin, a corral, and a sweat lodge. The Shaman of the local tribe lived in that cabin. He was the Elders' guardian and their only regular contact with the outside world. This cabin was Lisa's destination.

When the pair arrived at the cleared area, Lisa quietly and quickly sprinted across it to the cave entrance. Nela waited in the protection of the trees. Official policy was that no Elder would ever leave the butte without specific approval from the Council. One of the guards' duties was to watch the clear area and report any transgressions. This night was dark, however, and the guards were not known for carefully adhering to their duties. Lisa was only slightly worried.

She entered the passage and squeezed through the tunnel. When she came to the end of the tunnel, Lisa bumped into a large mesquite bush that covered the exit into the canyon. She was relieved that it wasn't a cactus.

Here she stopped to survey the canyon. She could see what appeared to be a dim light in the cabin window. There was one horse in the small corral. No one else appeared to be moving about. Lisa moved slowly along the east wall of the canyon toward the cabin. The sweat lodge would hide her approach from the cabin. When she reached the sweat lodge, she carefully peered out around it to make sure nothing had changed. All was still quiet. She slipped out past the lodge and made her way as quietly as possible to the cabin.

Lisa knocked softly on the cabin door, poised to immediately run back to the safety of the butte at the first sign of danger. There was a stirring inside. Then the door opened to reveal the silhouette of a tall, thin man, towering over Lisa. She was no expert on human physiology, but the man appeared young and muscular, with a full head of long black hair, darkish skin and was completely naked. To say the least, he was a completely intimidating figure.

The Shaman did not speak. Lisa summoned all her remaining courage. "Please, sir," she said, holding out the list of needs she and Nela had created, "we need this information. Can you get it for us?"

"We?" The Shaman's voice was deep and authoritative. He looked around for the rest of the 'we'.

"My partner and I ..." Lisa was almost quaking.

The Shaman took the paper and scanned it. "Come back in four days," he said evenly, went back into the cabin and closed the door.

Lisa hesitated for about half a second, then sprinted as fast as she could back to the safety of the butte and into the cover of the woods. It took several minutes before she was calm enough to tell Nela what had happened.

Lisa and Nela spent the next four days preparing their emigration proposal, leaving sufficient space to insert the information that would be forthcoming. As the day approached to meet again with the Shaman, their stress climbed to the critical level.

Nela was definitely worried. "What if he just ratted us out to the Council?"

"How could he do that?" Lisa was trying to sound more assured than she felt. "He is far too big to get into the butte."

"Maybe he has some way to contact the Council. We don't know for sure. You could be walking into a trap." At least Nela cared about Lisa.

"Look we're all ready to go, now. I'll just have to take that chance. I think he'll help us." And with that, Lisa left to keep her appointment with the Shaman.

The night wasn't quite as dark. There was a sliver of moon hovering above. Lisa made her way across the open space and through the exit into the canyon. Again she paused to survey the area. Same cabin, same corral, same horse. But the door to the cabin was open. Someone, the Shaman?, was sitting outside the cabin, puffing gently on a small pipe. There were no unusual sounds. Lisa decided there was no danger, so she left the protection of the cave and approached the Shaman as calmly as she could.

When she reached him, she could see that he was again naked. "Good evening, sir. Do you have the information we requested?" was the best she could muster.

The Shaman reached down and retrieved a piece of paper that had been nestling under his left foot and silently handed it to Lisa. "The next time you need my services, it might be better if you go through the Council." he said, quietly but sonorously.

Lisa almost fainted on the spot. Then, for the second time, she made a mad dash back into the butte and into the tree line. When she was safely back in the butte, Lisa decided that she would not tell Nela about the Shaman's last comment.

The next day Nela and Lisa completed their proposal with the information provided by the Shaman. When they reviewed it, it looked reasonable. Nela was still worried, but Lisa pointed out that the Shaman's duty was to protect the Elders. He surely would not have given them false information. That afternoon they went to the Council chamber to officially present the proposal to Ari-Alma. It was only then that the real waiting began.

They had to wait for Ari-Alma to read and approve of the request. They had to wait for Ari-Alma to present the proposal to the full Council. They had to wait while the Council considered the proposal and weighed it against any other simultaneous proposals. They had to wait for the Council to schedule a review session in which they asked any unresolved questions. They had to wait for a second consideration and then a final meeting in which the Council would render their verdict.

This was a tense time for the two Elders. Days and weeks passed. Nela had insisted on traveling to Arkansas in the late spring. That would be the ideal time to purchase the animals and the weather would be good long enough to get everything set up before winter arrived. It was already March. Time was running out.

It was near the Ides of March that Ari-Alma sent word to Nela that the questioning session would be the next day. Nela immediately dropped what she was doing and ran out of the Council chamber to find Lisa and tell her the good news. "Oh, piff!" was Lisa's only comment.

The next day there was a crowd in the Council chamber. Neither Nela nor Lisa had hid the fact that they were planning to emigrate. This was the first time that it was being done so publicly. Everyone wanted to be in on the process.

Nela and Lisa waited nervously for the questioning to begin. Ari-Alma was the first to speak on this issue.

"Since I have sponsored this petition for emigration," Ari-Alma began, "the Council has asked me to secure answers to their questions. The first question is: Where do you plan to acquire the funds necessary to execute your plan?"

Lisa almost gulped audibly, then answered, "We expect to pay the cost of the initial emigration from Colony funds … As have several previous emigrations."

"Second question: Are you sure that you will be able to raise goats as you propose?"

It was Nela's turn, "We have been studying material on animal husbandry that was in the supply bunker. We also expect to enlist the aid of other knowledgeable humans in the area of our farm. Particularly, from the source of the goats."

"Third question: What is your fallback position if your plan fails?"

Lisa almost bristled, "We will *not* fail!"

"Last question: Where did you acquire the monetary information you included in your proposal?"

Lisa and Nela just looked at each other. They actually had not anticipated this question. Lisa did gulp this time as she answered, "We got the information from a reliable source."

"Would you care to name this 'reliable source'?" Ari-Alma persisted.

Lisa had somewhat recovered. "No," she said, somewhat defiantly.

"Are you sure?" Was Ari-Alma hiding a smile?

Lisa had fully recovered her composure by now, though Nela wasn't quite there yet. Lisa simply sated, "Yes, I am sure."

The questioning was over. Now there would be more waiting. Would Lisa's refusal to name her source be sufficient grounds to refuse their proposal? Lisa and Nela both wondered, but they wondered silently.

At the end of March Nela and Lisa were summoned to the Council chamber. The Council was ready to announce their verdict on the petition to emigrate. Again, the chamber was crowded. Everyone wanted to know the result. All were wishing Lisa and Nela the best of luck. If they successfully emigrated it would serve as a lesson to many of the other Elders.

Again, Ari-Alma spoke for the Council. "On the petition of Nela and Lisa for emigration. The Council has arrived at a decision. It was not a unanimous decision. Two Council members voted to deny the petition."

At those words there was a quiet murmur among those in the audience. Nela and Lisa looked at each other, smiling broadly. That meant that the other three had voted 'yes'.

Ari-Alma continued, "Two Council members voted to approve the petition. One Council member abstained from voting."

There was dead silence in the room. No one could remember a tie vote before.

Ari-Alma was thoroughly enjoying this. She looked around the room smiling, primarily for her own benefit.

"There is a precedent that we follow when there is a tie in a vote." She stopped for a small dramatic pause. This might be fun for Ari-Alma, but it was agony for everyone else, especially Lisa and Nela!

"The last time this happened, we sought a deciding opinion from an unnamed, but reliable source. We also followed that procedure in this case." There was another small dramatic pause. "That source voted in favor of the petition."

For a moment the audience remained silent. Then it sank in. The petition had been approved. The Elders proceeded to violate every rule of protocol in the Council chamber and erupted into shouts of congratulations.

For their part, Lisa and Nela were very subdued. If it were even possible it might be said that they had very red-faces.

The celebration moved outside the Council chambers. The Councilors gathered their records and went to their respective quarters. As Ari-Mara passed Ari Alma, she paused for a moment.

"Alma, Do you really think that this emigration is not going to work?" she asked.

"I do have my doubts," Alma answered.

"Then that's why you didn't vote in favor of it." Mara sounded legitimately concerned.

"I admire Lisa's and Nela's creativity in preparing their plan," Mara continued. "I think they should be given a chance to carry it off."

"Creativity is fine," Alma said, "but that alone isn't what makes a good emigrant."

"What do you think is essential?" Mara asked.

"I would rather see a strong pioneering spirit," Alma explained, "a combination of optimism and energy and just plain guts. Lisa and Nela may have the creativity and energy, but I don't see the optimism and guts."

"You may be right," Mara admitted. "How do you see this ending?"

"I think they will be back within a year," Alma said, with just a touch of sadness.

"Well, we'll see," Mara was pensive. "Maybe we should consider preparing another pair to take control of the assets – just in case."

Chapter 3

The World of Humans

Having their petition to emigrate approved was one thing, actually getting out of the butte was another. But now Lisa and Nela could take advantage of official guidance. Ari-Alma took on the chore of getting them safely on their way.

The first step was a series of classes taught by the various Councilors. Neither Lisa nor Nela had ever left the butte for any extended time. To live successfully among the humans they had many lessons to learn.

First and foremost was clothing. Ari-Unna helped them go through the supply bunker to select appropriate attire. While among the humans they would have to mask their white skin, their dark eyes, their hands and feet. Long dresses with long sleeves and high necks would be essential. Also, shoes and gloves. There wasn't much that could be done with the face. A wig and dark glasses would have to suffice.

When Lisa started to protest about the clothing, especially the wig, Ari-Unna insisted, reminding them that they must be able to blend in among the humans. She took them over to a mirror resting against the wall.

"Look at yourselves," she cautioned. "Beautiful white, unblemished skin all over. Even the so-called 'white' humans have colored skin. You are completely hairless. Humans are mammals; they are distinguished by being hairy, all over. Their eyes are white with a colored ring around the pupil. Our visible eyes are mostly pupil and are completely black. Your nose and ears are passable, but you will have to use a colored lipstick to disguise you mouths. No, if you are to move freely among the humans, you will have to disguise yourselves completely in suitable attire."

Lisa and Nela looked at each other. Who knew things were going to be so complicated. Resignedly, they listened to, and obeyed, Ari-Unna's instructions.

Lisa and Nela also had to have a story which would make sense to the more gullible humans. Ari-Unna provided one that other Elders had successfully used. They would be traveling as ex-nuns who had acquired some odd disease while serving in Africa. A 'disease' from Africa usually caused the average human to back off and not get too curious.

"If the human is still curious," Ari-Unna said with a sly smile, "just mention leprosy. Most humans know nothing about it except that it is disfiguring and lethal. That should do it."

Once the clothing had been selected, Ari-Alma took over to instruct the intrepid travelers on how to travel.

"You will be less noticed if you travel by bus," Ari-Alma explained. "A bus is a large land vehicle, sort of like a tube, in which people are placed in rows of seats. Two seats together on either side of a central aisle. It will be hot, stuffy and smelly. When you get on a bus, be sure that you always sit together. You will be traveling overnight, so be sure that one of you is always awake."

"How long will the trip actually take?" Lisa asked.

"Probably about two days," Ari-Alma answered. "We'll discuss the details later."

Then she went on to explain about staying in a hotel, taking public transportation, using the telephone.

"You can find almost anything you need in a telephone directory with yellow pages," Ari-Alma told them." She also explained about area codes and ZIP codes.

Ari-Mina taught Lisa and Nela about money and methods of payment. The two Elders would be using cash money, most of the time. But they would also be carrying a large amount of gold to be used to purchase the farm.

There was much more instruction for Lisa and Nela: how to avoid eating in restaurants, how to conduct themselves around humans, how to use the humans' sanitary facilities, how to use telephones, how to avoid the police and hospitals, and much more. The instruction lasted for an entire week.

By the end of the week, Lisa and Nela heads were awash with data. But the Elder brain did not work the same way the human brain worked. All of the information that had been pushed on the two Elders was duly stored for later recall. The two Elders would not have to worry about forgetting any of it. When they needed any of the information, they simply had to intentionally recall it.

Then it was time to actually begin their journey. Ari-Alma had secured two satchels from the supply bunker. In each of them she packed some twenty-one pounds of gold bars. In one of them she packed fungus taken from the cave in the north end of the butte. She also included two large bottles of pure river water. In the other she packed the spare clothes Lisa and Nela would need and about $10,000 in hundred-dollar bills. She left room for the personal articles and the paperwork the two would need on the trip.

Lisa and Nela were suddenly summoned to the Council chambers one evening.

"It is time for you to leave," Ari-Alma explained when they arrived. "It is much safer for us to travel at night. The darkness helps disguise our features. A friend will pick you up at Grey Wolf's cabin and drive you to the bus station in Winton. There you will purchase tickets to Little Rock. Are there any last questions?"

"Grey Wolf?" asked Lisa.

"That is the name of the 'reliable source' you consulted," Ari-Alma replied.

"Oh," was all Lisa could come up with.

"You mean we are leaving now?" Nela's worries were beginning to surface.

"You are expected at Grey Wolf's cabin in twenty minutes. Don't be late or you may miss your ride. It is a long walk to Winton and an even longer walk to Little Rock."

"But, how do we pay for everything?"

"You will find the amount you requested in your petition in the two valises," Ari-Alma explained. "Whatever you do, never let any human see how much money you are carrying. And be sure not to let those valises out of your control. Now, unless there are more questions, it is time for you to be off."

Lisa and Nela were sent off to dress for the journey and to gather their personal belongings.

As the sun went down behind the west wall of the butte, they returned to the Council chambers to collect their valises, where their friends were gathered to wish them farewell.

"Your friends may accompany you to the butte exit," Ari-Alma told them.

When they arrived at the exit, good-byes were exchanged and the two squeezed through the cave with their valises, bidding farewell, forever, to the butte and the Elder colony. Lisa and Nela were off on their great adventure.

Grey Wolf was waiting for them at his cabin. Tonight, however, he was wearing a head band, leather pants and vest. Lisa and Nela barely had time to greet him before they heard a raucous noise and a strange vehicle turned into the canyon entrance.

The 'strange vehicle' was well known on the reservation. It was a left-over Korean War vintage Jeep. It belonged to the reservation sheriff who kept it in perfect running condition. It was equipped with a blue light and a scabbard for the sheriff's rifle, a .30 caliber carbine, also of Korean War vintage.

"This is Sheriff Johnny Eagle," Grey Wolf introduced Lisa and Nela to the driver, a tall man dressed in cowboy hat and boots with a flannel shirt and blue jeans. He appeared to be older than Grey Wolf and somewhat stouter in girth. "He and his trusty steed will drive you to Winton."

Then Grey Wolf became serious and in a deep, sonorous tone reminded them, "Be advised: we are the only two humans who know of the existence of the Elders or the secret of this butte. You are both charged to keep it that way. Under no circumstances are you ever to tell any other human about yourselves or about the butte. Do you understand?!"

Somewhat shocked, Lisa and Nela each nodded in agreement.

"Then it is time for you to leave," Grey Wolf's voice softened and became friendly. "May you have a safe and fruitful journey."

The two climbed into the back of the sheriff's Jeep with their valises and rode off into the night. The wild ride to the Winton bus station took less than a half-hour.

The bus station was a small, somewhat dingy looking building next to a service station. It contained two old benches and a couple of vending machines. It was brightly lit but, except for a clerk behind the counter, it was completely deserted. Sheriff Eagle dropped Lisa and Nela off in the parking lot and drove the Jeep over to the side of the building. Lisa and Nela looked around warily. They were now all alone among the world of humans.

Nela went to the ticket counter and inquired as to the cost of two tickets to Little Rock. With information in hand she returned to Lisa who was waiting outside with the valises. They extracted the proper amount of money and Nela returned to purchase the tickets. Then they waited, somewhat nervously, for the bus to arrive. It was only slightly late.

When the bus did arrive, The two Elders waited while a few passengers got off the bus, then they boarded with their valises and sought two seats together, as near the rear as possible. The bus only spent a few minutes in Winton. The driver soon boarded the bus and it departed the station. When it left, Sheriff Johnny restarted his 'trusty steed' and returned to his office in Wakulla.

According to the tickets, Lisa and Nela had to change busses three times: first in Tucson, then in El Paso and again in Dallas, Texas. It would still be dark in Tucson, but it would be early morning in El Paso and afternoon in Dallas. The bus to Tucson was a 'local' and would make several other stops to drop off or pick up passengers.

As Lisa and Nela settled back into their seats, Lisa wrinkled her nose.

"These humans really do stink," she muttered softly.

"I know," Lisa commiserated. Then she added, "Look! That passenger in front of us is doing something with the panel above his seat."

The two Elders watched as the passenger reached up and seemed to twist a knob on the panel over his seat. Then he settled back in his seat, apparently satisfied with his effort. Lisa looked up at the console over her seat. There was a light with a switch and a silver colored knob. She reached up, way up for a four foot tall Elder, took hold of the knob and twisted it.

As soon as she turned the knob, she felt a stream of air blowing through the knob. Then it dawned. That wasn't just a knob, it was a fresh air vent. She turned the vent until there was a strong breeze blowing down onto the seats. The incoming air wasn't the best smelling stuff she had ever experienced, but it was a lot better than concentrated human stink.

The Tucson terminal was larger, but just as dingy. Lisa and Nela had to wait about an hour for their next bus to arrive. They found space on a bench and managed to ignore all of the other passengers who were also traveling through Tucson.

Since this was their first real exposure to a group of humans, they took the time to observe them as closely as they dared. Even here in the terminal, Lisa thought that they smelled strangely. Nela thought that they didn't seem very friendly. Of course, they both agreed that the last thing they wanted to deal with was a nosy human who was getting too friendly.

Their bus finally arrived. It was much taller and larger than the little bus on which Lisa and Nela had arrived. When the two Elders tried to board the bus with their valises, the driver stopped them and strongly suggested that they store their bags in the area beneath the bus. Nela protested vehemently, clutching her bag close to her. Lisa resolved the situation by stepping forward, taking Nela's arm and helping her step up onto the bus. Lisa followed her so quickly that the driver was left stammering an apology. The two Elders again selected seats in the back of the bus and stowed their bags on the floor in front of their seats. There was plenty of room, as their feet didn't reach to the floor anyway.

So the Elders began their long cross-country journey. Lisa and Nela took turns sleeping, so someone would always be awake to watch the valises. They also read and swapped information on animal husbandry and farming to wile away the time. The bus made a rest stop in Lordsburg, New Mexico, but Lisa and Nela remained on board.

The first leg of their trip ended in El Paso, Texas. The bus they were on was continuing to San Antonio. Lisa and Nela were getting to be old hands at the transfer process. They went inside the terminal, which was small and somewhat dingy and dirty, to determine when the bus to Dallas would depart. They had over an hour to wait – if the bus was on time. All of the seats in the terminal were occupied and the human stench was almost unbearable, so Lisa and Nela went outside the building to wait.

It was cooler outside with a pleasant night breeze. It was also less smelly. The drawback was that it was quite dark. The Elders didn't mind the darkness; it was what the darkness might conceal that worried them. They tried to stay close to the door so that they could quickly dart back inside if danger warranted. Their worries were unfounded. With the exception of a couple of drunks who were no danger to anyone but themselves, their wait was uneventful.

The next bus was only about fifteen minutes late. Since Lisa and Nela were waiting outside, they easily made it to the head of the boarding line. The sun was about to rise in the east when the two Elders boarded the bus and secured two seats together in the rear. They indulged in a quick bite of fungus and a sip of water while the buss was still at the terminal.

As they left the terminal, they had a glimpse of the multi-cultural city of El Paso before the bus took on the barren expanse of west Texas. Lisa was enthralled by the changing scenery. She claimed the window seat and spent many of the daylight hours just staring out the window.

Occasionally, another passenger would try to engage them in conversation, but Nela had come up with a sure-fire conversation ender. She and Lisa were two nuns who were being reassigned to a new hospital and were under a vow of silence. Somehow, the inquiring passenger never seemed to notice that Nela was saying this.

The bus made two short stops on the way to Dallas so passengers could stretch their legs or get something to eat. But the larger buses had a small closet in the rear for the collection of human waste matter. After her first use of the facility, Nela agreed with Lisa's opinion that humans smelled. Their odor was not only strange but in some cases downright disagreeable.

Some twelve hours after they started, the bus rolled into the Dallas-Ft Worth area. Both Lisa and Nela had been impressed by the size and complexity of the human cities they had passed through. But nothing compared to the Dallas-Ft. Worth area. Mile after mile of houses, buildings and humans, not to mention the cars and trucks. They were arriving on a Saturday evening, but the amount of movement about the two cities was astonishing to Lisa and Nela. It was like a nightmare come true for the two Elders. They were just beginning to get a glimmer of the expanse of the planet and the number of humans it supported.

Lisa and Nela had to change buses again in Dallas. This time the terminal was large and relatively clean. There were many busses sitting in the loading/unloading area. They looked at the indicated destinations of some of them as they made their way to the waiting room. None were going to Little Rock. Once in the waiting room, they discovered that the bus to Little Rock would not leave for another two hours.

To kill time they decided to visit the café adjacent to the terminal. They each ordered a large glass of milk and spent the time watching the humans as they bustled about both inside and outside the terminal.

"Can you imagine such a vast array of dress?" Lisa marveled. "No wonder we can get by in these outrageous outfits."

"I wish we could just pitch them off and be ourselves again." Nela lamented. "This wig is horribly uncomfortable!"

"Not yet," Lisa warned. "Maybe when we find a place to stay in Little Rock."

Eventually, the bus to Little Rock was announced over the speakers in the terminal. Lisa and Nela gathered their valises and prepared for the last leg of their journey.

Chapter 4

Welcome to Arkansas

Very early the next morning, their bus pulled into Little Rock. Lisa and Nela disembarked and looked around. The sun was shining around the tall buildings, but it was definitely cooler than Arizona. The next step was to find a place to stay. They consulted the ticket agent, and decided on the Riverfront Hotel. It was only a few blocks from the bus depot and there was nobody out so early in the morning to see the two Elders toting their valises down the sidewalk.

There were virtually no cars on the street and the weather was pleasant. In ten minutes they had negotiated the distance to the hotel. It was a rather large building surrounded by trees and other greenery. There were many cars in the parking lot. From the upper floors it would offer a nice view of the river to the south. Lisa and Nela made their way to the front door, which opened at their approach.

The lobby was empty. The desk clerk barely raised an eyebrow when they walked up to his desk and asked for a room. Lisa almost choked when she heard the rate for a room. They had a large amount of money, but they couldn't afford to spend it all in one week at the hotel. Nela reverted to her nun story and described Lisa and herself as two traveling nuns who had taken a vow of poverty and were virtually penniless.

The desk clerk looked them over suspiciously. He obviously noted their dress, or lack thereof, that they had arrived on foot and that the valises they were carrying were absolutely ancient. Still, he could not give a room away at no cost. In the end, he said he would allow Lisa and Nela to have a room at only $50 per night.

That was still a lot of money, but the two Elders agreed that the cost and discomfort of trying to find some other place to stay would be just as excessive. They told the clerk they would take the room.

The clerk pushed forward a registration form and a pen. Lisa and Nela just stared at it. No one had briefed them on this little detail. Nela picked up the pen and started with the first entry: Name. "Lisa and Nela," she wrote. Next came: Address. The two Elders just looked at each other. They couldn't say anything about where they came from. Then Lisa had a brainstorm. "Riverfront Hotel", she wrote. Then she pushed the form back to the clerk, highly satisfied with her effort.

The clerk took one look at the forms and was almost apoplectic. 'I have to have your full name and where you came from." he demanded.

This time, Nela had the brainstorm. She added the word "Elder" after their names. But neither could come up with a better address. They had promised Grey Wolf that they would never reveal their point of origin. After a couple of tense moments, Lisa reached down to one of the valises and extracted a $100 bill. She placed that on the registration form and pushed it back to the clerk, saying, "Will two days' payment suffice?"

The clerk thought it over for a moment, saw more potential guests coming in the front door and handed them a small piece of plastic, told them the room number and welcomed them to the Riverfront Hotel.

Lisa and Nela found the room easily enough, but it took them a few more minutes to figure out how that piece of plastic unlocked the door. The room was nice enough: a single large bed, dresser with lamp and TV, bathroom, but no window.

"Too bad there isn't a view," Lisa sounded a bit disappointed.

"Apparently you have to pay extra for a view," Nela said, somewhat pointedly. "But remember, we wanted to save our money."

Once settled in the room, the first thing Lisa and Nela did was remove their wigs and clothing.

"Aah! That feels sooo good!" Lisa sighed as she put her wig on the desk. Nela was only a few seconds behind her. They hung their dresses in the closet and flexed their muscles as though they had just put off a great weight. While exploring the room, Nela found a little tag hanging on the door handle. It said, "Do Not Disturb". Its purpose was obvious; she gleefully hung the tag on the outside door handle.

Then Lisa and Nela immediately thought of looking for a real estate agent. It took a few minutes for Lisa to search the room and find a telephone book in a drawer. She took it to the bed and opened it to the yellow pages The two Elders found several possibilities listed in the phone book, and tried calling a few numbers. They got no answer at any number they dialed.

Nela checked the clock in the room. It was still morning. Someone should be at work. She looked at Lisa who just shook her head. For a minute, the two Elders were quite puzzled, then Lisa brightened. "When did we leave the Butte?" she asked.

"About 8:00 PM," Nela answered, still puzzled.

"No. What day?" Lisa persisted.

Nela had to think a bit. "Friday…" she replied, Then she realized what the problem was, and smiled right back at Lisa. "And today is Sunday. Humans don't usually work on Sunday."

There was really no point to making more calls until Monday, so the two settled in as best they could. There was nothing on television that interested them. Lisa even tried reading the Gideon Bible she found in the drawer with the phone book, but that was worse than television. They nibbled on a little fungus and went over their plans for developing the farm. They looked in the phonebook for possible providers of goats and chickens. They found nothing of merit.

Morning found them well-rested and ready to find a farm: a nice small plot of land in the country with a house and barn. Unfortunately, Little Rock wasn't quite ready for them. At first no agent they called could even come close to meeting their requirements. There were big farms, and bigger farms. But it seemed there were no small farms complete with house and barn anywhere in the surrounding country. The two Elders were beginning to get discouraged. From what they had read, there should be something in the vicinity.

One of the agents they called surprisingly said he could pick them up and take them out to see "the perfect farm". Lisa and Nela agreed to meet with him at 2:00 PM that afternoon in front of the hotel.

The Elders struggled back into their clothes and fixed the wigs carefully back on their heads. They were standing outside in front of the hotel when the agent drove up. He was driving a large vehicle, the likes of which neither Elder had ever seen.

The agent got out of the vehicle and came around to introduce himself and open the door for Lisa and Nela. Climbing up into the vehicle was an exercise Lisa had not anticipated, especially with the long dress and wig on. She handed the valise with the money to Nela and did her best. Once she was in the vehicle, she took the valise back from Nela and encouraged her to enjoy the experience. The agent was most personable as he helped her into the car.

As they drove off the agent explained that this was a new Army vehicle called a 'HumVee'. He had secured it in a test to determine how well the vehicle would perform in open country. As they were driving he kept up a constant line of talk about how well the farm would fit their needs, how really cheap it was and that he could even provide them with a herd of dairy cows if they wanted.

They were on the road for just over an hour and well out into the country south of Little Rock when the agent pulled into a driveway and stopped at a gate. Before Lisa or Nela could stop him, the agent jumped out of the car and unlocked the gate. Then he was back in the car driving onto the property. The farm did indeed have a house: a large house about 200 hundred yards down the entrance road. Behind the house, also many yards away, were at least two large outbuildings. One of these appeared to be a barn.

When the agent came to a stop in front of the house, Lisa managed to stop his constant babble long enough to tell him that this was far too large a property to be of any interest to her and Nela. He attempted to protest, but the two Elders insisted that they return to

Little Rock. Even after he leaped out of the car to show them the house, they remained steadfastly seated in the car. He eventually got the message. The trip back to Little passed in welcome silence.

On Tuesday morning the two Elders met with another agent who also assured them he had the perfect farm. This time they traveled more to the west. Again the farm they were shown was entirely too large for their purpose or their pocketbook. At least they had a chance to see something of rural Arkansas.

Lisa and Nela were beginning to feel desperate. They could not afford to continue living in an expensive hotel with nothing positive to show for it. so they kept on calling agents. Whenever an agent seemed too energetic in pushing a farm onto them, they were less eager to jump on the bandwagon. They started demanding pictures and facts on the property before they would budge out of the hotel room. They collected many pictures, none of which was what they wanted.

When the last name in the phone book failed to come up with anything appropriate, Nela told him that they had exhausted the phone book and asked him outright if there was anyone in the area who dealt with the kind of property they wanted. Amazingly, he suggested that she call "Old Maud Booth" and gave her the number.

Chapter 5

Maud Takes Charge

It was Lisa's turn to place the call. Maud Booth answered with a cheery, "Hello!" Being a bit taken aback by the unprofessional way in which she answered the phone, Lisa asked if she were in the real estate business. The response was even more surprising, "Used to be in the business, but I retired some years back."

"Oh," Lisa said, somewhat despondently. "We were told you could help us find a small farm. We've tried every real estate agent in the phone book. None of them could even come close."

Maud continued to surprise, "Well, I have been known to turn a property or two from time to time, just for fun and profit. Suppose you tell me what you're looking for."

"We want a small farm," Lisa explained, "on which we can raise a few goats and maybe some chickens. A farm house, maybe a small barn for the winter. Some privacy would be good. It doesn't have to be in perfect condition."

At that last comment Nela gave Lisa a dirty look, and whispered, "Not too imperfect!"

Maud was silent for a few seconds. Lisa was afraid she was going to say no, too. Then she suddenly sprang to life. "What say I stop by and show you what I can do for you? Where you staying?"

Lisa told her they were at the Riverfront Hotel and Maud said she would be by in fifteen minutes and to meet her out front. Before Lisa could ask how they would recognize her, Maud had hung up.

Nela, who had been listening in on the conversation, stared at Lisa with a questioning look. Lisa just shrugged.

The two Elders quickly got dressed and Nela grabbed the valise with the money. In fifteen minutes they were waiting outside the front door of the hotel. But waiting for what?

Suddenly in a rush of sound and color, a huge red car turned off the street into the hotel driveway and skidded to a halt right in front of the two startled Elders.

The meeting was spectacular! Lisa and Nela just stood there, totally transfixed. Maud Booth leaned over and pushed open the door of the bright red Cadillac convertible, and gaily announced, "Welcome to Little Rock!"

Maud was an older woman of undeterminable size or shape. She wore a simple, multi-colored cotton dress that draped loosely about her and sturdy walking shoes. She had salt-and-pepper hair that was partially pinned and partially blowing in the wind and bright red horned-rimmed glasses. She was, in one word, a mess. But she exuded happiness and was apparently sufficiently self-confident she did not need to worry about her appearance.

When Lisa and Nela just stood there staring at the site, Maud encouraged them "Well, you want to see your new farm or not?" The two exchanged glances and scrambled into the car, Nela still clutching the critical valise.

Maud took off through the traffic, scaring the pants off any vehicle that had the misfortune of venturing into her path. As she drove, she recounted and verified what the two Elders were looking for: a small plot of land in the country with a house and barn and water and grass to support a few goats. Lisa verified Maud's understanding, while trying desperately to keep her wig in place.

Maud's route took them out of Little Rock toward the northwest. There were several twists and turns and the two Elders were soon completely lost. The city gave way to forest land and foothills. It was obvious that Maud knew where she was going and was wasting no time in getting there.

They were on a narrow country road that wound through a collection of fields and trees. Then Maud turned onto a dirt road that had a 'Dead End' sign posted at the intersection. After passing a couple of mailboxes, Maud pulled over to the side of the road.

"So, what do you think?" Maud said. "Can I pick 'em or what?"

Lisa and Nela took a second to get their bearings. Along the road to the right was a line of greenery – shrubs and bushes of some sort, not well tended. There was a dirt driveway with a mailbox beside it. It led back along a row of trees and bushes to some buildings about fifty feet away that were not clearly discernable.

"Let's go have a closer look," Maud suggested.

They left the car on the road. Maud unlocked the chain holding a somewhat lopsided metal gate closed and they walked along the driveway. The house was a two-story wood structure. It had been painted white at one time, but had grayed over the years since. Across the front of the house was a broad porch, perfectly suited to watching the night sky. As they neared the house, a small barn could be seen to the left behind the house. An old barbed wire fence appeared to border the property. The two Elders couldn't really tell how complete the fence might be as they were walking in, because the property seemed to be completely bounded by trees. There was a green ground cover of some sort. Perhaps goats would like it.

Maud retrieved the house key from a lockbox and opened the door. Inside, the house was still partially furnished. It was musty and dusty, and had a few cobwebs scattered about. There was a large carpet in what appeared to be the living room. It was generally dirty and had a large stain in the middle of it. Otherwise, the house seemed solid and in good repair. There were two bedrooms and a bath upstairs. Downstairs was a kitchen, dining room and living room. Although the pump was not turned on, Maud assured them that there was running water from a well located behind the house.

Looking out the kitchen window, Nela asked, "What is that?"

Maud joined her, then ventured, "I think that was the grow-house."

Nela and Lisa both looked at Maud quizzically, so she hesitatingly elaborated, "The last people in this house were drug dealers. Some years ago there was a disagreement between them and some other dealers. They were all murdered, right here in this house. I think some of those stains on the floor might be leftover evidence.

No one has wanted to buy this place since. So, if you would like to look somewhere else, I'll understand ..."

"I'd like to take a look around," Lisa said.

Leaving Maud to relax in the living room, Lisa and Nela proceeded to examine the property from front to back. They discovered a small pond near the back of the property. They talked over as many pros and cons as they could think of on the walk back to the house.

They stopped to look at the well and the remains of the grow-house. The grow-house was in pieces; the frame was still standing, but it had been completely gutted and mostly demolished.

Nela squinched her eyes really hard. "I can almost see a chicken coop here," she said. "With a wire fence to keep out predators." Lisa looked at the pile of scrap wood and marveled at Nela's ability to see the future.

As they approached the back door of the house, Nela pulled Lisa over to the side. There, leaning against the house, were two wooden doors. Lisa grabbed onto one of the doors and lifted it open. A short flight of stairs led down into the darkness.

"Basement?" queried Lisa.

"There was no basement door inside the house," Nela said. "Maybe a fallout shelter?"

"Tornado shelter?" Lisa suggested.

"No, 'grow' room!" said Nela, hefting the valise she was still carrying. They both laughed at the thought.

The two Elders then rejoined Maud in the house.

"Well, what's your verdict?" Maud asked. "Want to go back to Little Rock now?"

"What is the asking price?" Lisa asked.

Maud wasn't really ready for that question. She paused for a second before she answered, "$250,000."

Nela countered, "This place will need a lot of work. What will the owners take?"

Maud thought for a bit and offered, "225".

Lisa entered the auction with "200 flat - hard money," then she paused for a moment, remembering their original instructions and added, "if it passes a building inspection and title search."

Maud initially frowned at the low figure, then she slowly looked around the living room where she had been waiting, and finally, grinning from ear to ear, she announced, "Sold!"

Maud drove Lisa and Nela back to the hotel where they waited impatiently for several days while the necessary paperwork was drawn up, the deed examined and the property inspected. Once all that had been done, there were additional days waiting while the telephone and electricity were connected and the water was turned on.

Maud had provided a list of phone numbers for people the Elders might want to talk to. Nela spent her time contacting a goat breeder and securing a small herd to be transported to the property. Lisa found a handyman who could do some rudimentary repairs.

Maud had kept in touch with the Lisa and Nela and was feeling a bit hurt that they never accepted any of her invitations to dinner or drinks. But she eventually relented, and brought a notary to their hotel room when it was time to sign the final papers. When the two walked into the room, Maud got her second surprise. There, sitting on the dresser, was a pile of gold ingots.

Maud stopped in her tracks. The notary, who had seen a lot of things before, just whistled.

"You know, I sort of expected a check," Maud said warily.

"Seventeen pounds of gold ingots," Lisa explained. "Roughly $210,000 at the going rate. That should be enough for the farm, conversion charges and a tip for your services."

"I'm sorry, but we don't trust banks," Nela added with a slight smile.

After the signing, Maud drove the two out to their new farm. When they got there, Maud turned over the keys and removed the lockbox. With many thanks from the two Elders, she remounted her red charger and sped off into the distance.

Chapter 6

The Farm

As soon as Maud was gone, Lisa and Nela removed their wigs and clothes and exhilarated in their new 'colony'. Their homestead was sufficiently hidden from the roadway that they would no longer need to wear the hated disguises any longer. Unless, of course, some human was coming to visit. Then, only one of them would have to dress up.

Lisa's first task after moving to the farm was to call the handyman back to make a few alterations. He created an entry from the bottom of the kitchen larder into the tornado shelter. Then she had the man remount and reinforce the doors to the shelter. Finally, the handyman installed a slow drip line at the top of one wall in the shelter. He really questioned this, stating that the water would just turn the dirt floor into mud. But Lisa persisted and the work was done. When the handyman left, still shaking his head, Nela and Lisa emptied all of the remaining fungus out of the valises and attached it near the top of the wall below the drip line. Once in position, it would absorb the moisture and begin to grow and flourish.

Their first purchase was a pair of wooden rocking chairs for the front porch. A Little Rock furniture store agreed to deliver them, for a fee. As soon as they were in place they became Lisa's and Nela's favorite resting place after a day's work on the farm. The two Elders greatly enjoyed being out in the cool of the evening air once again, watching the beautiful colors of the sky at sunset and the wonderful display of the stars. They were again out in the country, far away from the lights of human habitation.

In fact, they had not seen any other signs of life in the area while Maud had been driving them around. Lisa and Nela speculated that were truly alone out in the boondocks of Arkansas.

The two Elders made a thorough inspection of the farm's boundaries. As they suspected, the farm was bounded by barbed wire fence on all sides. Some of the fencing was hidden by overgrowth or trees, but it all seemed to be intact and serviceable. At one point on the west side, Nela thought she heard some animal sounds. The two listened carefully, but there were no more sounds.

Lisa called the goat breeder's number and told him they were ready to receive the goats. The goat breeder came and looked over the land and the barn. He pronounced it quite suitable for the animals. Then he gave Nela and Lisa a short course on the care and feeding of goats. He also put them in touch with a local feed store that could handle their future needs.

Lisa had intended for the goats to provide milk for the forthcoming children, and to augment everyone's fungus diet. Beyond that, whatever milk she and Lena didn't consume could be made into cheese and sold for a small profit. She had stipulated that the female goats be milk producers.

While they were waiting for the goats to arrive, Nela explained her scathingly brilliant idea. She would convert the old "grow house" into a chicken coop. "Fresh eggs," she pointed out. "We can even sell them at the farmers' market I saw back in that little town Maud drove us through."

"What do we need money for, now?" Lisa asked. "I checked our stash and we still have over $200,000."

"That won't last forever," cautioned Nela. "We haven't even had a chance to start building our colony. Children will increase cost. And what if something happens to the goats – or to the fungus? And what about a vehicle? It's a long walk to town."

"Touché," was the best response Lisa could come up with.

While Lisa was waiting for the goats, she kept herself busy cleaning out the barn. For her part, Nela tackled the old grow house. It had been a dilapidated wooden shed about twenty feet long. Sometime after the shooting, the insides had apparently been torn out and the illegal plants hauled away. She searched through the pile of scrap wood for useful boards. The unusable trash was set aside for the fireplace. She also drew up some rough sketches of what she wanted the new chicken coop to be like.

The goats arrived a couple of days later. For their part, the goats took a look around the farm and begrudgingly dubbed it satisfactory. After the goats had settled in, Lisa approached one nanny with bucket in hand. She had received some initial instruction, but had no practical experience in milking goats or any other animal. When she attempted to milk a goat, the fun began. Over went the pail, over went Lisa and off went the goat. Undaunted by one failure, Lisa tried again. This time only the pail went over. After several attempts, Lisa succeeded in getting a little milk in the pail. There would have to be much more practice in the days to come.

Nela continued her project of converting what was left of the old 'grow house' into a chicken coop. The roof had holes in it and needed patching, the door was missing, and the floor was filthy, but most of the walls were sound. Nela first set about cleaning out the debris.

She pulled the remaining old tables out into the yard and hosed them down well. When they had dried, she moved them back inside and set to work building nesting areas. There were enough good scrap boards laying around to fashion fourteen nests. The final touch involved pulling up some of the long grass in the north 'pasture' and drying it out for nesting material.

Nela called the number for the feed store and inquired about getting some chickens. The store was able to provide the layers and a source for chicken feed. They could arrange a delivery in a few days.

The house was a different matter. It needed a good cleaning. That became Lisa's job when she wasn't chasing goats. She found an old broom and started sweeping. After several hours of sweeping, the floor was ready to be mopped. There was an old pail in the barn, but no mop or cleaner.

That required a call to a hardware store in the nearest town. When asked if they would deliver to the farm, the response was an immediate laugh. Lisa tried explaining that no one at the farm had a driver's license and there was no vehicle available. The store manager was no longer laughing, but he still didn't deliver. Lisa tried the nun story. The manager was sympathetic, but he still didn't deliver.

While Lisa pondered this development, she set about cleaning as best she could with the broom and an old gunny sack she found in the barn. For the time being, she put a mattresses into each of the upstairs bedrooms. What was left of the two bedsteads, the box springs and all the other junk she relegated to the scrap pile.

Downstairs Lisa saved the kitchen table and two chairs, a small table in the hall to hold the phone and, in the living room, the sofa, TV, and another small table to hold it. Everything else went; the Elders simply had no need for it.

Then, with the house cleaned out, Lisa and Nela sat down at the kitchen table to draw up a list of supplies they needed. It wasn't a short list. They still needed cleaning supplies, linens, milk processing equipment - some pieces of which they could barely imagine, egg handling equipment, dishes and glasses for the kitchen. They did decide that they would postpone getting a frying pan for the chickens.

They still hadn't figured how they were going to manage getting all that stuff out to the farm.

That was going to be a set-back. Neither Lisa nor Nela had seriously considered the need for a vehicle. First there was the problem of getting a driver's license. Neither of the Elders knew how to drive a car. What about choosing a proper vehicle: a car? a truck? How would they even know if it was in good working condition? Even if they did, there was no way to even find a car to buy. There had to be another solution.

"Maybe a bicycle would work." Lisa wondered.

"But, how could they carry large bulky items on a bicycle?" Nela asked, pulling up her imaginary skirts with her hands. No, that was impractical.

"Maybe we could have the stuff mailed to us," Nela offered half-jokingly.

"That's not a bad idea," said Lisa. Nela looked at her as though she had lost her mind.

"Well, not mail," Lisa agreed. "But, suppose we contract for delivery services. We could find some young human with access to a vehicle and pay him, or her, to make deliveries to us on an as needed basis."

Nela considered the thought, "So how do we find such a person? And, if we do find someone, how do we arrange for payment?"

The two wandered out to the porch and their rocking chairs still pondering the problem. After much rocking and discussion, a plan took shape. Lisa went inside brought out the phone directory. She thumbed through the yellow pages and found what appeared to be the largest church in the local town (it had the largest ad) and dialed the number. She explained that she was house-bound and needed an honest person to run occasional errands for her, such as shopping.

"Could the church recommend such a person?" she asked the friendly voice on the other end.

"Let me see what we can do," the voice responded.

In ten minutes the phone rang. The call was from Jimmy Marten. He said the church had informed him of their need and he was prepared to do the job. Lisa explained the proposition. When she needed anything from town, she would call Jimmy with the list. He would pick up the items and deliver them to the farm. On he first trip she would reimburse Jimmy for the items he brought and give Jimmy a fee of ten dollars for the trip. She would also give Jimmy one hundred dollars to cover the cost of the next purchase. If she ever cancelled the service, the hundred dollars was Jimmy's to keep. Jimmy jumped at the chance and the deal was struck. Lisa got Jimmy's phone number and gave him their first list of cleaning supplies. Jimmy said he would pick them up and be out at the farm in an hour.

Jimmy was true to his word. Within an hour, an old Ford pickup pulled up at the farm gate. Jimmy was a young lad of eighteen, tall and thin, with a shock of sun bleached hair. He was dressed in jeans and a t-shirt that both looked work soiled. He had the requested products and the bills from the stores. Lisa, properly attired in dress and wig, met him at the gate where she accepted the items and paid over the funds as promised. Jimmy beamed when he saw the crisp new hundred-dollar bill. But, as he left, Lisa thought that he looked back at her momentarily with a curious expression.

Lisa brushed off the thought. "He's just a young boy," she thought to herself.

When Lisa carried the bags inside, she passed a mirror and glanced into it as she went by. Wig was in place, sun glasses on, shirt and skirt. "Oh, piff!" Her shirt was open at the collar and she wasn't wearing any socks! She was exposing far too much white skin. They were definitely going to have to be more careful.

The next few weeks were filled with work and learning. The one thing the two Elders learned above all else was that farming was hard work.

They also decided, that while chores would be shared, they should each be able to do all the various jobs. So, Lisa began coaching Nela on the proper way to milk a goat and how to convert the milk into cheese. That tornado shelter was becoming useful as a storage and processing center.

For her part, Nela completed work on the chicken coop and ordered the chickens and chicken feed from a local store. The clerk at the store said he could arrange delivery.

On the designated day of delivery, Lisa heard a yell from the gate, which the two Elders kept locked as a security measure. She quickly dressed, more carefully this time, and ran out to the gate

There was a woman dressed in faded blue jeans and a flannel shirt patiently waiting.

"Hi," she extended a friendly hand, "my name is Betty Foster. I live on the next farm - the last house on this road. The feed- and-seed store suggested that I bring your chickens and feed out to you. I've been in the chicken business for several years and might be able to give you some hints on how to get the most out of your birds."

Betty proved as good as her word. Lisa showed Betty to the new coop and shouted for Nela to join them as they passed the house. By the time Lisa and Betty had unloaded the feed, Nela arrived, properly attired. Nela and Betty unloaded the hens and placed them on the nests with a little feed to keep the happy. Then Lisa retired from the scene and let Nela learn all about raising chickens from Betty. They were at it for over an hour before Betty honked as she passed by the house on her way home. Lisa followed her out and secured the gate.

"I made a point of saving everything she said," Nela exclaimed as she sat down wearily at the kitchen table. "She even gave me her phone number, in case we need any additional help."

"Good," Lisa replied. "I think we have another chore to tend to. We really need some way to tell when there is a visitor at the gate."

"Okay," Nela said. "How do we go about that?"

"Some sort of a doorbell." Lisa answered somewhat unsurely. "I'll look into it."

First, Lisa tried the phone book. She could find no satisfactory entry for 'doorbell'. In desperation, she called Jimmy and told him of their need and asked if he had any suggestions. Jimmy said that he worked in the local hardware store and could come up with a solution. He would bring the necessary materials out the next evening and install it. Lisa was more than happy to accept his offer. Still, she wondered, would it be wise to let him into the house?

Jimmy showed up about six o'clock the next evening and honked as he arrived at the gate. Lisa dressed and went out to meet him. As she arrived at the gate, Jimmy was mounting a board with a buzzer on it to the fence post that secured the gate. There was room at the top of the board to post a message or instructions. Lisa unlocked the gate to let him in.

Jimmy had a roll of wire and several tools and other parts with him. He gave the tools and parts to Lisa while he unrolled the wire as the two walked toward the house. At the house, Jimmy mounted a loud bell high on the wall at the edge of the porch. Then he connected the bell to the house's power.

"If anyone presses the button at the gate," he announced, "The bell will ring once. If someone cuts the wires, it will not stop ringing. Just as a safety measure."

As Jimmy was leaving, after being paid for his services, he took the time to bury the wires from between the house and the gate. Lisa followed him out and locked the gate behind him. Then she tried the button. She could even hear the bell from the gate. She and Nela would be able to hear it wherever they were around the farm.

Slowly, a rhythm developed. Both Lisa and Nela learned how to milk the goats and care for the chickens. They each became well versed in every chore, well, almost everything.

And with that, our new gentlewomen farmers settled into their new home.

Chapter 7

The Town Talks

The town closest to the farm was Conly, Arkansas. It was a small country town. There was one prominent example of everything. One church (Baptist), one supermarket (Safeway), one bar (the Razorback), one feed store, one meat packing house, one hardware store, one drug store, one convenience store (Cumberland Farms).

The local men's club was the Masonic Lodge. There was a movie theater that showed old films on Friday and Saturday and a bingo hall that catered to the ladies in the afternoon and served as a Catholic church on Sunday. There was not a lot of excitement. So when two mysterious women showed up one day and bought the old Brown farm, the town was all agog.

Joe Higgins, who ran the gas station, had seen Maud Booth's distinctive Cadillac in the area recently. He called Maud and pumped her for information. All Maud would say was that the two women had purchased the old Brown place for cash and were going to farm it. That word 'cash' had a nice ring to it. The women's wealth was magnified every time Joe recounted the message.

Tom, over at the supermarket, added the information that they couldn't drive and ordered stuff to be delivered to the farm. He also mentioned that Jimmy Marten was the appointed currier. Reverend Briggs confirmed that they had called his church looking for an honest boy to make deliveries. The church had recommended Jimmy. At that point everyone focused on Jimmy.

At first, Jimmy could only confirm what the townsfolk already knew. He had a certain sense of honor that said he shouldn't tell tales about his employers.

The owner of the feed store said that he had supplied chickens and feed to the farm. That Betty Foster had been in that day and had

53

taken the order out to the farm. And they had reordered the feed, so they must be doing something right. When Betty Foster had stopped into the store recently she had mentioned that the women were planning on selling eggs and goat milk and cheese at the local farmers' market.

Eventually, Reverend Briggs mentioned on Sunday how the women had come to the church for help when they needed it and the ladies of the church decided it was high time to invite the two women to come visit the congregation and maybe join the church. At the least such a request might serve to clear up their status as ex-nuns.

"You know," Vivian said, "you're right. We should have paid them a visit long ago. Let's set up a visit for Monday. Who will go?"

"Henry and I will go," Jane replied. "We'll pick you and George up at 10:00 Monday morning."

So, on a sunny Monday morning, the two church couples set out for the Brown farm with the happy intent of visiting the farm and inviting the newcomers to visit their congregation. Henry made a wrong turn along the way, almost getting them stranded in a cow pasture, but in due time they arrived at the gate to the farm. Henry parked the car by the gate and the group got out to take a closer look.

They found the entry gate closed and locked. They walked along the fence as much as they could. They peeked and the peered through the foliage. At one point Vivian thought she saw someone moving about the farmyard. The others looked where she indicated, but there were too many trees and too much brush to get a good view. The small person dressed in white was an enigma that they could not explain. Maybe it was one of the nuns. Other than that sighting they had gained no further information.

"Supposedly, they can't drive," Jane commented. "Where would they go?"

Jane examined the gate more closely. "Looks like there's a bell," she announced.

"There *is* a bell," Vivian said, and pushed the button. A loud sound was heard from the direction of the farmhouse.

Then they waited. Almost ten minutes passed with no sign of activity.

"Maybe I ought to try again," Jane offered and poised her finger over the button.

"No, wait," George cautioned. "I think I see someone coming."

Indeed, Lisa had heard the bell. She wasn't expecting anyone, but she dressed as quickly as she could and came out to see who wanted to get in. She did not recognize any of the people standing at the gate.

"Can I help you?" Lisa asked as she approached the gate.

"We're from the Conly Baptist Church," Vivian began. "I believe you contacted us when you needed help. We'd like to invite you to visit our church."

Lisa was completely taken aback by the visitors and their proposal. This was another blasted new situation for which she had not been briefed. How in the world was she supposed to react? Best practice: be honest.

"I am afraid," she finally replied, "that my par ... uh, sister and I am not really interested in your kind offer. Thank you very much. We greatly appreciate your assistance in finding Jimmy Marten, but we are just not interested in visiting your church."

With that Lisa quickly spun around and returned to the farmhouse.

The four church members were stunned by Lisa's response. They had no recourse left but to get back into their car and drive back to Conly.

"My," Jane said when they were underway, "that was quite a blow off. Polite, but still a blow off. And did you get a look at that outfit she was wearing? Quite curious! Hardly suitable for farm work."

"I'm more curious," Vivian ventured, "about what she didn't say."

"What now?" George sighed. He knew his wife and her whims only too well.

"When she stuttered, right off the bat," Vivian explained, "I think she almost said, ' ... my partner and I ...'."

"Maybe she was about to say '... my pardner and I ...'" George interrupted, "and thought it was too western"

"Atta boy, George!" Henry couldn't resist. Then winced when Jane jabbed him with her elbow.

Reluctantly, they returned to Conly. On the way back they compared notes. On returning to the church, one of the ladies suggested calling the farm to see if they could arrange a future visit. Someone mentioned that they should have done that to start with. They called the operator, got the number of the farm and placed the call. No one answered the phone.

The conversation and speculation didn't stop when they returned to Conly. It became the new topic for town gossip. What did the woman at the farm almost say? Bob at the Safeway recalled the initial telephone call when someone at the farm said they were nuns. That fanned the flames even more. Perhaps they were Catholic and that's why they weren't interested in visiting the Baptist church. But are they nuns? Or *were* they nuns? Ex-nuns? That didn't seem feasible to most folks.

The townsfolk again started pestering Jimmy Marten for details. And he steadfastly refused to provide any titillating tales. But he did start to wonder. He remembered that first visit to the farm. The woman who was called "Lisa" had appeared rather strange. What he could see of her skin had been pale white. Just who or what were these strange people who had purchased the Brown farm?

The Reverend Jack Briggs was a tall man with a face that was just perfect for glowering from the pulpit. He had a sharp temper and did not take kindly to non-Christians in general. He didn't have any doubt as to what the women were. He had heard Vivian's comment about that little 'slip' at the farm. That made everything perfectly clear to him. The word 'partner' had been practically copyrighted by the gay community. Two women, living together on a farm, one of whom referred to themselves as 'partners'. And who didn't to have anything to do with the church. It was all so simple: they were homosexuals!

The Reverend saw this as the initial thrust of the gay invasion into Conly, and he knew just what to do about it. He would raise such an anti-gay fervor in town that they wouldn't be able to survive here. Eventually they would have to leave the area and they would tell the rest of their kind to look elsewhere for a place to live.

Accordingly, he planned his next sermon. He couldn't actually brand the women at the farm as lesbians, after all, he *could* be wrong. But he could also preach a scathing sermon about the evils of the gay community and the gay lifestyle. After that, he would just need a little more evidence.

When Reverend Briggs ascended to the pulpit the next Sunday, he started out with a few standard references to Deuteronomy. Then he continued with assertions the all homosexuals were an abomination to God. That they were all perverts and a danger to any Christian child. He invoked the images of Sodom and Gomorra and their destruction by God to prove that the homosexual practice of sodomy was against the laws of God. He even brought up the story of the Stonewall riot to illustrate the depths of depravity that the homosexual engaged in. He ranted on about the evil of homosexual practices without ever mentioning once that common Christian teaching encouraged his parishioners to love the sinner – even if they hated the sin.

After some forty minutes of this sort of rant the congregation was numb; but they knew to a person that they did not want any gay people in their town. With his initial mission accomplished, Reverend Briggs paused after the service to have a word with his son, Todd.

Todd was to be a senior at the local high school. He was a strong, athletic young man who participated in all sports, especially football and baseball. He was genuinely good looking, or so many of the girls thought. And he was devoted to his father. So when the Reverend suggested to Todd that he keep an ear out among his friends concerning the folk at the Brown farm, Todd knew well what he wanted.

Chapter 8

Betty Makes It Work

It wasn't long before Lisa and Nela became painfully aware that they had bitten off much more than they were capable of handling. Lisa no longer had any trouble getting milk out of the goats. In fact she had more milk than she could use. At first, it was just a little extra. Then it was a gallon extra. Now there were several gallons stored in the 'grow room' waiting to be made into cheese. Lisa couldn't process it fast enough.

Nela was faring no better. She didn't want the chickens confined to their nests. But she didn't realize that 'free range' meant just that. The chickens were everywhere and so were their eggs! The rooster couldn't even keep up with them. Both the Elders were afraid some nighttime predator would start attacking the wandering chickens and then migrate to the goats.

Nothing that Nela and Betty had discussed covered the current situation. They decided that it was time to consult again with their local expert. Lisa was elected to make the call, as she was usually the more sneakily diplomatic of the two.

Lisa dialed the operator and asked for the number of the Foster farm But the operator had a problem as to what the actual address might be. She had several 'Fosters', and could the caller provide a bit more information, please?

"Betty Foster," Lisa elaborated. But, the operator responded, all of her listings were under men's names. She didn't have a listing for 'Betty Foster'.

"The Foster farm at the end of Blue Skunk Road," Lisa insisted.

"I'm sorry," the operator replied, "but I don't have a map."

Lisa looked over at Nela. "Do you have the number she left here the last time she visited?" Nela just shook her head. Lisa glared at her, "I think you are enjoying this!" she growled.

A little more negotiation with the operator ensued before Lisa finally exploded.

"Look, you piffer, connect me with that farm or I'll crawl through this wire and melt all your circuits!" Lisa was fuming.

Two clicks later Bill Foster answered his phone with a cheery, "Hello?"

"Hello, this is your neighbor, Lisa. May I speak to Betty, please?" Lisa's voice had instantly returned to its pleasant, jovial self.

When Betty answered Lisa explained the problem. Then she added, "Look, Nela and I have never done anything like this before, but we really want to make a go of it. You were great to help us out before, and I don't want you to think we are trying to take advantage of you. Can we work out some sort of accommodation?"

Then there was more negotiation - how Lisa began to hate that peculiarly human trait. Finally, it was all worked out. Betty would sign on as a partner in the milk and egg sales and in turn would get the project up and running until Lisa and Nela were ready and able to take over.

Bright and early the next morning Betty was at the gate rarin' to get started. The very first thing Betty suggested was to pen up the chickens.

"I don't know why I didn't say anything about it the first time I was here," Betty apologized. "I'll go into town and get the necessary stuff. You do have some money don't you?"

Lisa went to get the money while Nela and Betty went out to measure the area the chickens would use. In a couple of hours, Betty returned from town with the requisite supplies.

As the three started setting out posts, Betty couldn't help but comment. "You don't plan to dig fence post holes and stretch wire in those dresses, do you?"

This caught Nela and Lisa off guard. When they were working around the farm they didn't wear any clothes at all, and it was never a problem. They could see that the dresses were going to be a real hindrance, but they didn't have a solution at hand. They didn't have any pants and they certainly couldn't take the dresses off with Betty around. And putting the fence up would require all three of them. Betty was almost a foot taller than the two Elders and was the only one of the three who could handle the six-foot tall roll of wire.

Everything came to an abrupt halt as the two Elders just stood there looking at each other.

"I'm sorry, Betty," Nela said. "This is all we have. And I don't think it would be appropriate for us to take them off."

"I'm the one who should be ashamed," Betty apologized, "I just didn't want you to tear them or get hurt tripping over them. I've seen you often enough to realize there is something different about you and it's none of my business what it is."

Now the two Elders were staring at Betty. How much did she know? What did she suspect?

When Betty saw Lisa and Nela staring at her, her face turned bright red. "Oh, damn!" she exclaimed, "now I really have opened my big mouth and stepped in it. I really am sorry! Maybe I should just go. ..."

"No! Wait!" Nela said to Betty, and she turned to Lisa.

"This may be our 'make or break' point," she whispered. "I think we can trust her, at least a little bit."

"Oh, right!" Lisa groaned. "Well, we've got enough money left to get home in style. If we survive."

Nela turned back to Betty, "You are right, we are different. We are albinos. While it is nothing we are ashamed of, and it's not

61

catching, some people react to our appearance with disgust or fear. So we keep ourselves covered to make normal communication easier."

"If you don't mind," Lisa added, "we will take our dresses off and get on with this job. All we ask is that you do not mention our condition to anyone. Not all people are as tolerant as you are."

Betty hesitated a moment and then replied, "Of course it is alright with me. And I promise I will not say a word about this." Privately, Betty was thinking, "No one would believe me, anyway!"

With that Lisa and Nela pulled off their dresses and set them aside. They kept the wigs, glasses, gloves and shoes securely in place, otherwise they were completely naked. Their white skin practically glowed in the sunlight.

"Oh, that feels good!" Lisa said. "Now let's get busy with that fence."

In a few minutes they were all busy digging post holes and setting the fence posts in position.

"Some people just use a four-foot fence," Betty explained as she dug another fence post hole. "That is all they really need. But I prefer a taller fence to keep the casual predators out. A six-footer will keep out most varmints, except for chicken hawks. And we don't have too many of them around here."

By the end of the day, the fence was up and the chickens were back on their nests. The three retired to the kitchen where they could plan future events. The two Elders put their dresses back on and all three settled down with some cold goat's milk as Betty told them about the local farmers' market.

"I go there every week," she said, "with whatever spare produce we have. I would be happy to stop by for your milk and eggs. We can split the proceeds 50-50."

"No " Lisa interjected. "We don't need the money as much as we need to get rid of extra stuff. Why don't you take 60%? At least for now. Later, we can renegotiate" Lisa almost winced when she used that word.

"That's okay with me," Betty nodded. "And if you should need anything on market day, just let me know. I will pick it up for you and take the cost out of your share of the proceeds."

Nela had been standing by the sink, and she now added her thoughts to the conversation. "Suppose we put our milk and eggs outside the gate on market day. That way you could just pick them up on your way by, and not have to wait or come inside the gate. Wouldn't that be easier?"

"Yes, it would," Betty agreed. "But what about your share of the sales?"

"Just leave the money in the mailbox and anything else just outside the gate on your way back", Lisa said.

"Are you sure it will be safe?" Betty asked.

"Who's going to come way out here to steal the mail and milk cans?" Nela asked. And they all laughed.

So it was agreed. Betty would loan them the necessary containers to start with and the Elders would buy one replacement each week. At that rate they would soon have all the supplies they needed and a source of income as well.

Betty told them to call her if they ever had any questions, reassured them that their secret was safe with her. She gathered up her tools and headed home.

Lisa followed Betty out to the gate and locked up behind her. When she returned to the house she joined Nela who had shed her clothes and wig and was quietly rocking on the front porch.

"We were sure lucky to find her " Nela mused.

"Yeah," Lisa answered settling into her chair.

The two Elders just sat quietly and gently rocked as the sky darkened and the stars came out. For the first time since leaving the Butte, it really looked as though their little colony had a future.

Chapter 9

Coming Together

Nela was the first to bring it up. She and Lisa were standing in the shower that evening, washing off the dust of the day. Lisa was taking her turn at the flow and Nela was standing behind her. Nela reached up and placed her hands on Lisa's shoulders, massaging gently. At first Lisa just stood still, then she gave a little groan. The massaging continued for a few minutes. Lisa slowly turned around to face Nela and they exchanged places under the flow. Lisa remained in front of Nela, with her hands on Nela's shoulders and returned the favor of a massage. Lisa's hands slowly descended to Nela's hips.

"Are we ready for this?" Nela asked quietly.

"I am," was Lisa's reply, softly whispered into Nela's right ear.

Lisa reached around Nela and turned off the water. Nela grabbed a towel and proceeded to dry both of them, patting and stroking in just the right places. The towel dropped to the floor as Nela and Lisa embraced each other. "Where?," whispered Lisa. Nela was facing the window and noted the star-studded sky. "The porch?" she suggested quietly.

The two moved quickly through the house, hand-in-hand to the front porch. The gate had been secured for the night, so there was no threat of interruption. The air was cool and the setting sun provided a brilliant display in the sky as Lisa and Nela sank down to the floor. They lay quietly side-by-side, nuzzling and slowly investigating each other's body. Eventually, their hands made their way to their inner thighs, at first stroking slowly, then faster and faster as the tension and pleasure built. At the peak of passion, a penis emerged from each Elder to impregnate the other. Two new Elders were conceived. Lisa and Nela remained on the porch, locked in a loving embrace for many hours. The colony was growing.

An Elder pregnancy is only partially similar to a human one. The fetus is smaller, the pregnancy only lasts for only six months and delivery is far easier. The mother's belly does expand enough that it is noticeable, but not so much as to incapacitate the mother. So Lisa and Nela being pregnant did not significantly disturb the routine on the farm.

Lisa and Nela were each in seventh heaven over the impending birth of their children. In her spare time, Lisa designed a special sling that would fit over one shoulder and cradle the baby while they were working.

One evening, the two sat down at the kitchen table to work out a plan of action. They would keep to their schedule of milking and feeding the chickens and gathering eggs. To save their strength, they would take turns churning half the milk into cheese. In their free time they would keep up with minor repairs. They also debated the merits of setting up a spare room as a nursery, or keeping the babies with them or sleeping separately. They finally decided to keep the babies with them at the beginning, then move them into a separate nursery as they grew older and more self-sufficient. That would perpetuate the separation of singles and couples that existed back in the butte.

One problem that had not been foreseen manifested itself after the first few months. The clothing that Lisa and Nela had brought with them was no longer large enough to completely hide their pregnancies. They still realized the need to be properly clothed when visitors arrived, but the dresses simply didn't fit and had significant gaposis. That only served to emphasize the pregnancies to any human visitors. And visitors there were. The two Elders did not give a second thought to what the humans might think. Unfortunately, they should have.

Jimmy now stopped by at least twice a month, as did Betty Foster, the neighbor who helped with the chickens and took the milk, cheese and eggs to market each week. Betty would not be a problem. After all, she had already seen them without their dresses and all had been well. Seeing that both of the Elders were pregnant would be a new experience, but Lisa and Nela were certain that

Betty would deal with that as well as she had dealt with the fence building project.

Jimmy was another matter. He was an unknown factor. He was younger. He was a male. (Would that matter?) They finally decided that they would just have to do the best they could and play it by ear.

They were much more concerned with possible problems associated with the impending birth. Before they left the butte they had been given phone numbers of other existing colonies. Lisa and Nela took turns calling each of the colonies to ask for information and suggestions.

There was no answer at the colony in New York, but the other three responded. The consensus was that there would not likely be any problems. None of the other colonies had experienced any. But they were equally adamant that, should a problem occur, Lisa and Nela should do the best they could. Under no circumstances were any humans to be called in to help. No one had any specific suggestions. All just said to let nature take its course.

When she hung up the last call, Lisa just snorted, "That was a perfect waste of time!"

"Not so fast," Nela replied. "Each one of them said that giving birth was no big deal. Maybe we ought to just go with that."

Lisa wasn't convinced, but had nothing better to offer.

"What about feeding?" Nela asked.

"With those slings I made, we can nurse on the go at first," Lisa suggested.

"Speaking of nursing," Nela mused. "my breasts are already becoming sensitive. I bumped into the coop door yesterday and it really hurt. I almost dropped the eggs." Lisa echoed her sentiments with a knowing nod.

That brought up another issue: what about diapers? They opted for cloth and Nela set up a clothesline between the house and the coop. At the proper time one of them would call Jimmy with an order for diapers and clothes pins. If no one had noted their change

66

in size by then, that would be positive proof that babies were brewing on the farm.

There was no calendar on the farm. Time just passed, as it usually does. So no one noted that six months had passed since that wonderful night of bliss. It was already late February and Spring was trying to blossom forth. Nela was out collecting the eggs when she felt a sudden and insistent squeeze within her belly. The sensation was strange. She had never felt anything like it before. It was several minutes before she realized what was happening. She ran back to the house without the eggs, yelling for Lisa as she went.

Lisa at the moment was occupied with a particularly petulant nanny. She heard Nela yell, and jerked a little too hard. The nanny let out a bleat and took off, spilling Lisa and the milk onto the ground. That spill triggered a spasm of pain. Lisa struggled to her feet and stumbled in the direction of Nela's yell.

The two arrived at the house simultaneously and headed for the bathtub. Somehow it seemed like a reasonable place to give birth. They filled the tub with water and took up positions at either end. Once they were in place, sitting in the tub facing each other, they just sat there looking at each other and laughing at their appearance. Then they sat back, relaxed completely and just let it happen. True to the information they had received, the babies came out easily and smoothly with only a modicum of discomfort.

When the babies were safely lying on towels on the bathroom floor, it was time to deal with the umbilical cords. Lisa and Nela shared a ball of twine and a pair of scissors. They each left a small piece of the cord on the baby and a small piece connected to their uterus. Those pieces would slough off in a few days.

.A quick check of the babies revealed that they were healthy and hungry. Nela and Lisa each picked up her respective baby and headed out to the front porch and the wonderful rocking chairs. They sat and rocked and fed their babies. Then they just sat and rocked and cuddled their babies. The colony had just doubled in number.

As they rocked, Nela was the first to broach the question. "Now that these little darlings are here, what are we going to call them?" Lisa offered, "Babyone and Babytwo?" Nela frowned.

"Alright," Lisa said, "I am naming mine, Anele – one who came from Nela."

"Even I know that isn't proper Eldertongue," Nela said quietly, thrilled at Lisa's tribute to her. "You could just turn it around and we would know what it meant."

"Enela, it is!" agreed Lisa.

"And I shall name mine, Elisa!" proclaimed Nela. "And so shall it be."

The two Elders spent the rest of that day sitting quietly with their babies, reflecting on the marvels of life.

The two babies, for all their innocence, turned life on the farm upside down. Now the new order of things was feed babies, do chores, feed babies, change diapers, deal with visitors, do chores, check on babies, ad infinitum. It took weeks to develop a reasonable schedule. And, just when Lisa and Nela thought they had things organized, the babies decided to change feeding and sleeping schedules.

The two new parents soon became completely frazzled. Lisa, in desperation, called one of the other colonies. She was given three valuable pieces of advice: congratulations, that's the way babies work, get over it. For some strange reason, Lisa did not feel any better.

Slowly, but surely, as time passed, things did start to improve on the farm; but trouble was brewing in town.

Chapter 10

Jimmy Gets an Eyeful

When the summer ended and the new school year began, Jimmy found himself in a real time crunch. He had enjoyed working at the hardware store over the summer. The money was good and the work not all that hard. He was also learning all about running the business. Now, he had to spend most of the day in school. He could still work at the store in the evening and on weekends, but his hours were greatly curtailed.

Just to make life more difficult, Jimmy also liked his frequent trips to the Elders' farm as their delivery boy. He especially liked the hundred dollar bonus he would get if they ever canceled the service. Being a fairly literal person, he was sure that he would not get to keep the money if *he* canceled. Since he did most of his deliveries in the evening and on weekends, he now had to choose between the store or the farm. Then there was time for homework. Jimmy was no straight-A student – he needed that study time.

Jimmy also had another problem. He was getting older and was now an accepted member of the gang of boys that hung out at the Razorback out on the highway. Jimmy didn't want to risk losing that privilege by not showing up to claim his seat at the table.

Speaking of the Razorback, the most popular and well-supported place in town was the Razorback Trough, the town bar. It was a typical small bar. There was music on weekends; sometimes it was even live. Smoking was permitted and spitting was tolerated. The one doing the spitting was encouraged to hit the spittoon. The bar featured peanuts, boiled eggs and, of course, pickled pigs feet. Simple sandwiches were available on demand. There was a pool table and a couple of pinball machines in the back. These were frequently in use during the evening hours. Almost every male in the town visited the bar at least once a week. Some were steady customers. Id's were not zealously checked.

Jimmy had a heart-to-heart talk with Mr. Morgan, the store owner. Ed Morgan had heard Reverend Briggs' sermon on the homosexual menace, but he wasn't convinced that the women at the farm were lesbians. He trusted Jimmy and didn't believe that Jimmy would support such people. He told Jimmy that he could take off a little time from the store to make deliveries to the farm. Mr. Morgan would just count it as community good will.

When Jimmy first explained his problem to Lisa and Nela, they agreed that, unless it was an emergency, Jimmy could limit his trips to weekends. It would not be a big deal. Jimmy thanked them and heaved a big sigh of relief. His school and work schedules would be manageable, with extra time available for a night or two at the Razorback.

Jimmy stopped in after work one day shortly after school started. He picked up a bottle of beer at the bar and went to a table in back where Todd and Eddie were sitting. They were discussing the upcoming football game as Jimmy settled in.

"That Morrison school is going to clobber us!" Eddie was proclaiming. "They are twice as big as we are. And they have money."

"Nonsense!" Todd proclaimed. "I'm playing quarterback. What do you think, Jimmy?"

"Gee, Todd, you're a great quarterback," Jimmy always tried to say what he thought Todd wanted to hear. He was too new at this game to be able to act independently.

"See?" Todd jeered at Eddie. Eddie just grimaced. Todd continued, "So, Jimmy, are you still making deliveries to those two women at the Brown farm?"

"Yes," Jimmy answered, "Once or twice a month." He really didn't care for the interrogation he always got from Todd, but he figured that was the cost for his seat at the table and just went along with it.

When Jimmy finished his beer he headed home to get a start on the week's homework.

Such was Jimmy's life through September and October. School and work and the Razorback during the week; work and homework and the occasional delivery to the farm on weekends. Then came Thanksgiving. Jimmy wanted to do something nice for Lisa and Nela to celebrate the holiday, so he purchased a small turkey for them and delivered it, quite unexpectedly, on Wednesday evening.

The two Elders were surprised when the gate bell went off announcing a delivery. They looked at each other questioningly; then Lisa ran to get her wig and shoes and struggle into her dress. She hastened out to the gate, doing her best not to slip on the snow which now covered their farm. (The two Elders had come to hate shoes as an insidious invention.) She found Jimmy waiting at the gate.

"Happy Thanksgiving!" Jimmy announced. "I have brought you a little something for the holiday. I hope you enjoy it." Jimmy's speech slowed down toward the end as he caught sight of Lisa's dress gaping open about he middle. It was also lifted up a bit in front, exposing Lisa's white ankles.

Lisa thanked Jimmy for his kind gift and then, perhaps a little too quickly, suggested that he get home and out of the cold. For his part, Jimmy remained silent, but he couldn't help but consider Lisa's comment. He was wearing a heavy jacket and pants while she had only the thin dress she had worn last summer. And she was worried about him being cold?

True to his code of ethics, Jimmy never mentioned the Thanksgiving experience to Todd. Jimmy reasoned that he shouldn't gossip about his employers and he wasn't really all that sure about what he *had* seen.

In December, Jimmy repeated his Thanksgiving misadventure. He again showed up on a Saturday evening, just before Christmas with a card and a few small gifts for Lisa and Nela. He again rang the gate bell. This time Nela came out to meet him. (Jimmy had learned to recognize the two Elders by their wigs, the dresses they wore and a slight difference in their voices.) Even in the dark of evening, he could see that her dress was gaping apart over her belly and was hiked considerably in front, exposing white ankles.

Nela thanked Jimmy for his thoughtfulness and encouraged him to get home, out of the cold. Again, Jimmy noted that Nela was clad only in a thin dress while he was again wearing a heavy coat and gloves.

Jimmy gave all this some serious thought. The next time he dropped into the Razorback for a beer with Todd, and Todd asked the usual questions, Jimmy hesitated just a bit too long.

"Whoa! What's up?" Todd asked. "Have you seen something unusual?"

"Well," Jimmy procrastinated, "Were you thinking that the two women out at the farm were homosexuals?"

"That's the general idea," Todd asserted; Eddie snickered "What have you seen?"

"Well," Jimmy was still battling his sense of loyalty toward his employers. After a serious internal struggle, he decided that he might be able to defuse the situation. He asked his own question, "Do homosexuals get pregnant?"

"Not hardly!" Todd responded and he and Eddie broke out in absolute guffaws. "Don't tell me ...!"

"Yes!" Jimmy interrupted. "I think they are both pregnant." That assertion stopped the conversation, momentarily. Jimmy took a deep swig of his beer.

Todd and Eddie looked at each other. "You sure about that?" Eddie asked.

"I'm sure," Jimmy said. "Their bellies are definitely much bigger."

"Jeanie, get over here," called to his girlfriend, who was sitting at a nearby table with Eddie's girlfriend.

Jeanie pulled up a chair at the boys' table and sat down.

"Look," Todd asked her, "give me a thumbnail sketch of pregnancy."

"What, you skipped sex-ed, too?" Jeanie replied. "It starts the usual way ..."

"Don't get smart!" Todd snarled. "When does a woman start to get big?"

"It depends on the woman ..." Jeanie started then stopped as she saw Todd getting mad. "It does depend on the woman," Jeanie insisted. Then she asked in defense, "How long is a guy's cock?" Todd was taken aback by this question, but before he could react violently, Jeanie continued, "It depends, doesn't it?"

"Okay! Okay!", Todd relaxed a little. "I just want to know when she starts showing. What's average?"

"Well, I didn't take detailed notes in class, and I have no personal experience, but I would venture a guess that the average woman would begin to show openly around the 4th to 6th month."

"Thank you," Todd said with phony sincerity. "Now go back to Mary."

When Jeanie had left the table, Todd did some quick calculating. "They arrived some time in June, didn't they?" Todd asked no one in particular. He continued muttering to himself, "November, October, September, August, July, June." Then he looked up, straight at Jimmy.

"What?" Jimmy exclaimed, following Todd's train of thought. "No way!"

"Okay," Todd said, "them who?"

"Maybe it happened just before they got here", Eddie offered. "They might be late bloomers."

"Yeah", Jimmy offered, anxious to get out of the spotlight. "Remember, they originally said they had been nuns. Maybe they were thrown out because they got pregnant and ended up here."

"Yeah," Todd said, "maybe."

Jimmy quickly finished his beer and bade the other two good-night. "What have I done?" he wondered to himself.

Chapter 11

The Town Talks, Again

Despite the paucity of information about the area's new inhabitants, or possibly because of it, the women continued to be the hot topic of conversation at church, at the bingo parlor and at the Masonic Lodge. Especially at the church, the rumor persisted that the women were ex-nuns. Somehow that made them more exotic.

As the months passed the rumors came and went. The more grandiose the rumor, the more certain everyone was that it was true. At first it was all good clean fun at the expense of people who could not, or would not, explain themselves.

It was shortly after Christmas that Todd told his father about his conversation with Jimmy. His father thanked Todd for the news. He also warned Todd to keep the news to himself and to keep his ears open for any additional information.

Members of the congregation kept insisting that it was strange that two women would take over the farm. The meaning behind that statement was lost in translation. The topic came up again at the January pot-luck. There were two women alone at the farm. No men were in evidence. They were being very secretive about what was going on. Maybe this was really something that needed looking into. The Chief of Police was called into the discussion, but he pointed out that the farm was not in his jurisdiction. And so far as he knew, no law had been broken.

The Chief was also a member of the Masonic Lodge. At the January Lodge meeting he just happened to mention the concern of the local church matrons. Of course, he again stated that the farm was out of his jurisdiction, and there was no evidence of any wrongdoing. But the seed had been planted.

The Police Chief was a regular customer at the Razorback bar, so there was very little trouble. Anyone caught fighting, displaying a weapon or seriously drunk was offered a night's lodging in the town jail.

The women at the Brown farm were a frequent topic of conversation at the Razorback. One night, Jimmy Marten dropped in to share a beer with some of his friends. He happened to overhear another patron proposing that the two women were "lezzies". "That's not possible," he interjected without really thinking. "The last time I went out there both of them had either become very fat or very pregnant."

The conversation in the bar came to a sudden halt. Everyone looked over at Jimmy. "So are you getting a little on the side?" someone shouted.

Now, Jimmy, who had only wanted to defend his benefactors, found himself in real trouble. There were demands for more information. When Jimmy professed that he didn't know any more, he was not believed. All he could do was repeat his belief, based on his own observations, that the women were pregnant.

Several of the patrons wondered out loud how that could be possible. There were no men known to be living at the farm. A deed search when the women had first arrived had shown that the owners were Lisa and Nela Elder. If one or both of them was pregnant, who was the sperm donor? Obviously, there had to be a sperm donor. But, wait, another interjected, What about artificial insemination? Some wag suggested the goats were somehow involved, but he was generally ignored.

Since it was generally known that the women had no car and could not drive – then, no matter how impractical, using artificial insemination just supported the notion that they were indeed lesbians.

The talk tapered off as closing time approached, but it did not go away. The subject popped up again in church. Reverend Briggs even delivered a sermon on marriage being decreed by God and the evils of pregnancy out of wedlock. He got rave reviews from the church members.

This new development was also the subject of much conversation in the Masonic Lodge. Several of the members posed questions on what the Lodge could do to rid the area of this scourge. Some suggested contacting the state Grand Lodge for guidance. No one had an answer. But everyone had a comment.

Jimmy and Todd found themselves in the middle of the situation. Todd's father kept urging him to come up with more information about the 'perverts'. Everyone was hounding Jimmy for additional information on the women at the farm. Nothing was forthcoming until February.

Early in February Jimmy got a call from the farm asking him to include two dozen cloth diapers, diaper pins and clothes pins in the next delivery to the farm. Jimmy told the gang at the Razorback about the pending diaper delivery. That settled the pregnancy issue. But it did little to determine the source of the pregnancies. Everyone now focused on who did the dirty deed.

When Jimmy made the delivery to the farm he was met by a much slimmer Nela, whose dress now fit as it had originally. Considering that he was handing her the diapers, Jimmy felt it would be appropriate to congratulate her on the birth.

"I suppose you are now a proud parent," he said. "Did Dr. Clark assist in the delivery?"

"No, " Nela answered, "we did not need any assistance." She accepted the delivery and change, gave Jimmy another hundred-dollar bill and locked the gate.

"Gee," Jimmy thought to himself as he went back to his truck, "she didn't even blush." As young as he was, Jimmy understood how girls would often blush when dealing with personal issues. It was curious that Nela hadn't done that. Her skin had remained quite pale. Perhaps she was much older than Jimmy had originally thought. Or was she just different?

That news also made the rounds of the town. Everyone had an opinion, but no one knew what to do about it. Some even wondered why anything needed to be done. They were generally ignored. One person at the church thought they ought to call one of the gossip magazines, such as the 'National News', about the situation. Maybe they could investigate and resolve the whole issue.

Reverend Briggs quickly squelched those ideas. He did not fancy a national news organization trying to dig up dirt around the town. They might well find more of interest than just the farm. He did sit down one evening and have a long talk with Todd.

"You know, Todd, " her began, "this whole affair about the farm is getting out of hand. I believe it is high time to put the situation to rest.

"There is only so much I can do from the pulpit. I have tried to convince the people that the situation is so unsavory that they should ignore it in the name of God. But they continue to follow the Devil's path and revel in all that is unholy."

"They are just having a little fun, Pop" Todd responded. "This is a pretty dull town."

"This is supposed to be a Christian town," the Reverend almost shouted. "I have worked for years to teach these people right from wrong. Now, these two woman enter the picture and everyone is off following the Devil's path. I've got to do something about that, but I just don't know what."

Todd was silent for a few minutes. Then he said, "Well, Pop, maybe I can do something."

"You?" his father questioned. "If you have an answer, I would surely like to hear it."

"Maybe," Todd said, "We should just encourage them to leave this area."

"How are you going to do that?" his father asked. "Just politely walk up to the door and say, 'Would you please leave the area; you are causing the town people to misbehave.'? I won't stand for anything illegal; especially not if it involves the church."

"Don't worry, Pop," Todd said with a slight smirk, "there are ways of doing such things. Just leave it to me."

Reverend Briggs was not overly happy with the way that conversation had ended. He thought he knew his son well enough to trust him with a little mischief. He just had to ensure that things didn't get out hand in the bargain.

Chapter 12

Night Visitors

Todd Briggs was a senior at the local high school. He had just finished the season as their star football player. He had grown up in Conly, spending every Wednesday night and Sunday morning in the town's Baptist church. His father, the Reverend Briggs, was a Past Master of the local Masonic Lodge. Todd and some of his buddies had just become old enough to begin visiting the Razorback Inn. They were frequent customers on Friday and Saturday nights.

One night, Todd and his buds were sitting around a table downing a pitcher of beer and discussing the merits of a game of pool when Jimmy came in and joined the group at the table. When Jimmy was asked in passing how the pregnancies were coming along, he dropped a bombshell. "At least one of them is no longer pregnant," he said as he sipped his beer. His friends clamored for more details, but Jimmy just said that he had delivered a bunch of diapers to the farm. He had only seen one of the women and she was definitely no longer pregnant.

All this agitation got Todd's attention. He had promised his father that he would do something about the women at the farm. Perhaps it was time to take action. While conversation moved off in another direction, Todd began to focus on the problem of the farm. If the women at the farm were really lesbians they were perverts, the scourge of the earth, an abomination to God, destined to go to Hell. If they were defrocked nuns who had gotten pregnant out of wedlock, they were little better. People like that deserved to be eliminated before they could infect the whole town. When he brought this thought to the table, his buddies, feeling no pain from the effects of the beer, agreed heartily.

Life after football was too boring for Todd. Basketball was okay, but it wasn't his thing. He craved some excitement. Perhaps this could be the answer. At any rate he would be meeting his promise to his father and doing the town a service. "Why don't we go out for a little ride?" he asked.

The group was too large to fit in a car, and Todd didn't know the way to the farm, so he and his comrades piled into the old pickup truck that belonged to Jimmy. Jimmy drove, Todd sat in front and the rest rode into the back. In a few minutes they were headed out of town toward the farm.

It was nearly midnight when they reached the farm. The house and grounds were dark. The gate was securely locked. Todd suggested that they could just climb over the gate and investigate more closely. Eddie was more cautious. "What about the goats they raise? I don't see any of them, but it looks like the barn door's open. I don't relish tangling with an angry billy in the dark."

Todd was half way over the gate, but he stopped and backed down slowly. "Yeah, we don't know if they have any guard dogs..." he said slowly. "What about that, Jimmy?"

"I've never seen or heard any," Jimmy said. "But don't take my word for it."

Todd squinted toward the farmhouse. Coming all the way out here and just going home did not sit well. "We have any protection?" he asked.

A quick reply came out of the darkness, "I have a Trojan in my pocket." There were a few titters, but Todd was not pleased. He scowled in the direction of the comment.

"There's some pipe behind the seat in the truck," Jimmy offered. "I was going to use it for a well project."

This was better. "The well!," Todd thought. He and Jimmy investigated and returned with a four-foot section of cast iron pipe. "Let's go," Todd ordered.

He led the boys over the fence and they proceeded quietly along the driveway toward the house. There was a sliver of moon out that night and the farm had no lighting so they carefully watched where they stepped and kept an eye out for a wandering goat. They reached the house safely and moved silently around it to the well in back.

Jimmy and Eddie had worked with wells before. But Jimmy did not really want to have anything to do with harming his employers, so Eddie pointed out the well's vulnerable points. They managed to turn off the water flow and disable the well.

"That ought to discourage them," Todd exclaimed. "Now let's get out of here."

The boys quickly retraced their steps and piled into the back of the truck. Todd had another idea. He got in back of the truck with the pipe and directed Jimmy to drive down the road a ways. When Jimmy turned around and headed back toward the farm, Todd motioned him to drive close to the gate. As they passed by, Jimmy dutifully swung to the left and Todd braced himself and wielded the iron pipe. There was a very satisfying thud as the mailbox went flying into the ditch. With whoops and hollers, the boys returned to town.

With the birth of Enela and Elisa, life on the farm was forming a new pattern. Now, the babies had to be fed morning and evening, and given water in between feedings. Lisa and Nela had given the babies their morning feeding, changed diapers and were about to head out to do the farm chores, when a loud, steady beeping caught their attention. The noise was coming from the road in front of the farm. It did not go away. Lisa passed Enela to Nela, quickly dressed and ran out the front door.

As Lisa got to the gate, she could see the mail truck sitting at the side of the road. The mailman usually honked when he had a delivered a package, just as a courtesy, but he had never stayed around leaning on the horn. "What's up, Mac?" Lisa yelled out as she unlocked the gate.

"I can't just leave mail by the side of the road," Mac said. "I have to have a legal mailbox to stuff it in."

"So?" Lisa came up beside the truck. "Ow!" she stubbed her foot on … what? It was a twisted mass of metal, but it did bare a faint resemblance to her mailbox. She stepped gingerly around it and saw the bare post where the box had been attached.

"What happened?" she gasped.

"I wasn't here, so I'm sure I don't know. I only know that if you want me to deliver the mail, you've got to have an approved box for me to put it in. And that ain't it." Mac wasn't really as grouchy as he tried to sound, and Lisa knew it. "But, if I were to offer an unofficial guess, I'd say that some kids took a baseball bat to the old one. They used to do that right often, but I haven't seen any mailbox attacks in a long time."

"Can you at least give me today's mail?," Lisa asked.

"Yeah, but I can't do this on a daily basis. I'll have them hold your mail at the PO until you call and tell them that you have a new box installed. Here's the number." Mac handed her two feed catalogues and the PO's card and headed on down the road.

Nela was waiting anxiously for Lisa to return. Neither of them could explain why all of a sudden someone wanted to knock over their mailbox. It was an inconvenience and an unnecessary cost, but did no serious harm. Nela suggested that if it happened once, it was likely to happen again. The question was – how to deal with this new phenomenon. After pondering for a few minutes, Lisa had a sly grin. She reached for the Little Rock phone book, looked up an entry and placed a call. If she ordered some supplies, would they deliver? Fine! Payment on delivery? Tomorrow? Good. Lisa proceeded to place her order.

"Can you handle the kids and the farm without me for a couple of days?" Lisa asked Nela. "Of course," was the swift answer; but Nela was looking very quizzically at Lisa.

When Lisa went to fill a water bottle at the sink, she got another shock. There was no water. There was also no leak. Nela ran upstairs to check the bathroom while Lisa looked in the 'grow' room. There was no water anywhere.

"We have to have water!" Nela exclaimed. "What could have happened?"

"One guess!" Lisa replied hastily as she sped out the back door to the well.

The well had indeed very neatly been sabotaged. Another telephone call to a well company claiming an emergency elicited a polite response, but no scheduled appointment. Lisa was on the phone and she was mad enough to chew the wires themselves. She told the well company that it was a matter of life and death for the farm; if the company didn't come and fix the well, the next call she made would be to the police to implicate the company in murder and then to an attorney to sue the company for enough damages to buy a bigger, better farm.

Whether or not the man on the other end of the line was laughing his head off, he agreed to send a crew out that afternoon.

Chapter 13

The Plot Thickens

When Mac returned from his mail rounds, he usually retired to the Razorback for a sandwich and a beer. He had heard the conversations that had been circulating regarding the Brown Farm. Tonight, he actually had something to contribute. He waited patiently for the more vociferous patrons to arrive.

When the time was ripe, Mac wormed his way into the conversation, "You know, there is something going on out at the Brown farm." Heads turned his way. Everyone was anxious to hear the latest news. Mac explained how he had found the mailbox smashed that morning when he tried to deliver the mail. "Someone is out to harass those women," he expounded. Todd, sitting at a nearby table, just grinned quietly to himself.

Then Mac looked over at Jimmy and asked, "You ever notice anything unusual about those women?" Jimmy was a bit puzzled, "There are a lot of queer things about them. What do you have in mind?" As soon as he said it, Jim was sorry he had used the word "queer". But he breathed easier when no one took the bait.

"What about their skin color?" Mac asked. The men around the table looked at each other. Several commented to no good purpose. No one had heard anything about an unusual skin color. The women had been so thoroughly covered up, there was little skin to observe. They were generally thought just to be Caucasian.

Mac continued. "I got a good look at one of them today and she was white all right, pure white. Not like you or me. We're not really white. We're more like a very light shade of brown. She was as white as a sheet of paper. No color at all." Mac waited while the others digested this piece of information

There was a lot of muttering and head-shaking, but Mac held fast to his story. Todd was listening carefully, working out his next move. He knew it would take a few days to replace the mailbox. Then it would be time to pay the farm another visit. He could keep doing this until June graduation. It was almost as much fun as the weekly football games had been.

In a few days, Todd called the post office to inquire if the Brown farm was again receiving mail. Being assured that it was, he called his friends for an evening at the Razorback. At first Jimmy was not in favor of another visit to the farm, but, after a few beers and the encouragement of others in the group, he relented. As in the previous visit the boys piled into the back of Jimmy's pickup while he drove. This time, however, Todd retrieved a couple of baseball bats from his car before they departed the bar.

It was again near midnight when the group arrived at the farm. The night was overcast and moonless. The darkness was pervasive. They drove slowly down the road, looking carefully through the trees to the farm. There were no lights and no movement. Anticipation was clearly building as they turned around and drove slowly back toward the farm. Still there was no sign of activity.

"OK, let's do it," Todd urged. He stood up in the back with a baseball bat in hand. The truck made another pass by and turned for the final run. This time the truck gathered speed as it approached the farm. Jim braced himself and, at the last minute, swung with all his might. The bat stopped abruptly in mid swing and was jerked from his grip. Todd fell to the bed of the truck groaning in agony. Jimmy didn't waste any time in getting back to town. No one really knew what had happened. Todd refused to go to the hospital, so his friends helped him to get home. They would compare notes in a few days when Todd was feeling better.

Lisa, who had risen as soon as she heard the truck outside, had gone out to the area of the gate and hidden herself well in the bushes. She had witnessed the entire fiasco. When the truck had departed, she went out to examine her mailbox. On the ground was a very well chewed up baseball bat. The mailbox, sturdily constructed from an abundance of concrete block, rebar and bricks, was untouched. Lisa just smiled and went back to bed, taking the remains of the bat with her.

The next day, knowing in all likelihood that such action would be futile, she called the county sheriff and suggested that she had something he might be interested in.

Chapter 14

Todd Plots Revenge

It took Todd over a week to recover sufficiently from all the aches and sprains he suffered when he attacked the mailbox to venture out of his house. While he was laid up lamenting his stupidity and cursing those damned perverts, his anger only grew. His father tried his best to intercede and thanked Todd for his efforts. But Todd would have none of it. He was now determined to force those women out of Conly one way or another.

Todd had suffered one defeat in front of his friends; he was not about to suffer another. As soon as he was able he called a strategy meeting at the Razorback.

When Todd and his friends were comfortably seated around a table in the back room with drinks in hand, Todd leaned in and said, "Guys, it is time to teach those lezzies a lesson they won't ever forget. One that will drive them out of our area forever!"

His comments were set forth in such strident terms and with such obvious hatred, that neither Jimmy nor any other friend dared to question them. Just to ensure their compliance, Jim was quick to point out that God hated faggots. They were an abomination in His eyes. And the same went for whores who had sex out of wedlock. No one around here would care a whit if they were chased away.

And that was his plan: to drive those two "women" out of Conly and out of Arkansas. He reminded them of his father's scathing sermon of only a few weeks ago. Slowly they all came around to Todd's point of view.

"So," Jimmy asked, "just how are we going to force these people to leave the area?"

"I've got a plan," Todd assured them. "It will take a few days to get everything ready. I can't do this alone; you will each have a role to play. I guarantee that it will be spectacular. And it will drive those queers out of here once and for all."

"We aren't going to get into trouble are we?" Bob asked.

"If everyone does his part, no one will ever know what happened," Todd warned. "We're just going to make it too hot around here for them to stay," Todd said with a sly grin.

"Here's what we're going to do. Eddie, Ted and Jimmy, I want you to scrounge up at least 24 empty whisky or wine bottles, liter size. Be subtle, don't get them all at one place. If anyone asks why you need them, just say that the women out at the farm have requested them. You don't know why. Box them up and store them in Jimmy's truck. And Jimmy, keep you gas tank filled. Then all of you stand by and wait for my call. I'll call you and tell you when and where to meet me. Be prepared to come immediately whenever I call. Needless to say, you are not to mention this to anyone."

"Why don't I get in on the action?" Bob was whining again.

"Because I need someone to cause a diversionary action and you are it." Todd explained. "You are the most important actor in this little drama. Without you this will never come off."

Bob was not really convinced, but agreed to his role in the plot.

Todd ordered another round of beers and them sent them on their way, with a strong warning not to do anything weird during the next week.

Todd has his own tasks before him. If what he had in mind worked, he would need a good alibi. The sheriff had already been around asking questions about a certain baseball bat that had been found on the road in front of the farm. It supposedly had his fingerprints on it and traces of concrete from the mailbox. That was easy to explain away. Sure, Todd had used the bat for batting practice. The perp, who had apparently used it on the mailbox, had worn gloves. Anyone could have taken from the school dugout. The sheriff had to admit he didn't have a case.

This time, it would be different. Todd couldn't afford any mistakes. He called up Jeanie.

"Hey, Jeanie, it's Todd. Why don't we get together next Friday. Burgers and a movie?"

"And why should I bother with you?" was the caustic reply.

"Because we're friends, Jeanie. You know I still like you."

"I'm not impressed. I remember sitting around the Razorback at one table while you and your boyfriends were gathered about another one having a great time."

"No 'boyfriends' this time. Just you and me. Burgers and a movie at the Strand. What do you say?"

A little more negotiating and Jeanie agreed to the date.

Todd's father had asked him to mow the yard. Todd decided that this was a perfect time to do that. He got the mower out of the garage and drained the gas out of the old gallon can into the new five-gallon gas can he had purchased. He put both cans in the trunk of his car and went to the downtown gas station. He made a show of filling the gallon can. Telling everyone about having to mow the yard.

Then Todd drove off to an out-of-town gas station and quietly filled the five-gallon container. Then he went home and mowed the yard.

Todd remembered the bat and carefully cleaned all of his finger prints off the large gas can. If someone should question the odor of gas in the trunk of his car, Todd could point to his visit to the local gas station and the damp and smelly one-gallon can in his father's garage.

He was ready. All he had to do was bide his time.

Chapter 15

Fire!

On Friday, Todd was ready. At six PM he called the guys and told them to meet him in the church parking lot at 10:00. He cautioned them to turn off engines and lights when they arrived. He told Bob to meet him on the side street by the theater.

He picked Jeanie up at seven at they went out to eat at the drive-in on the highway north of town. After a filling meal of hamburgers and shakes they returned to town in time for the late show. Todd chose to park on the street in front of the theater. He made a slight commotion while buying tickets at the box office. Then he and Jeanie went into the theater, bought some popcorn and drinks, and found some seats near the rear of the theater. Todd opted to sit on the aisle.

When the picture began, Todd put his arm around Jeanie. He snuggled close, but not too close. He let his other hand wander a little, but not too much. All was going perfectly. Then about thirty minutes into the first movie, Todd suddenly claimed stomach upset and quickly left his seat in search of a restroom.

The theater lobby was already dark and empty. Todd easily slipped out the door of the theater and made his way to the side street where Bob was waiting. They drove directly to the church parking lot.

"Bob," Todd said, "I told you I had a special job for you. I want you to go to a payphone up on Highway 10. At 10:30 exactly call the county fire department and tell them there is a house on fire just east of the state forest. Make it sound real! Like you're panicking. Then hang up. Don't answer any questions. Then just go home. Remember, everything else tonight depends on that call. Don't fail me!" Bob didn't quite understand, but he nodded conspiratorially and drove off toward the highway.

The church was on a side street. The parking lot was on the back of the church, out of sight of any casual passers-by. Todd got there a little early so he could arrange the position of the vehicles and retrieve the five-gallon can of gas he had stored in the church's shed. As the cars came into the lot he had them positioned around Jimmy's pickup so that it was effectively hidden from view.

"Bring the bottles," Todd ordered and knelt down behind the pickup. One by one they filled the bottles by siphoning gas from the can. Eddie was given the job of tearing up a couple of old sheets to stuff in the mouths of the bottles. When they were all filled and back in their boxes, they went back into the pickup.

"Now drive over to my place and park your cars," Todd told the others. "Jimmy and I will be by in a few minutes to pick you up. If anyone should ask, we were just having a late night bull session."

"What about your folks?"

"They are off to Little Rock for a conference. They won't be home until tomorrow. Now Let's roll!"

In a matter of minutes, the parking lot cleared. Everyone headed for Todd's house. Todd got in Jimmy's truck and followed them. In a matter of minutes they were all in Jimmy's truck, headed to the Brown farm.

Bob headed out route 10 looking for a suitable pay phone. He spotted one at a convenience store, pulled in to a spot as far from the door as possible and waited for the appointed time. The longer he waited, the more he doubted in this was the right thing to do. He didn't know exactly what Todd had in mind, but if it involved misdirecting the fire department, it didn't feel right. As 10:30 approached, Bob was torn. If he failed Todd his life would be miserable; not that it was so great now. If he made the call, and sent the fire department on a wild goose chase in the wrong direction He could get into serious trouble. Bob was getting a headache just from thinking about it. Best not to think. Bob picked up the phone, dialed the operator and asked for the fire department.

After calling the fire department, Bob dialed the operator again and asked for the Brown farm.

Jimmy had the truck at the Brown farm at 10:30 sharp. Todd jumped out, cut the chain on the gate and swung it wide open. Jimmy quietly backed the truck into the yard and turned it around. Everyone piled out and Todd distributed the bottles and matches. Jimmy would head for the back of the house. Eddie would take the left side of the house and Ted would take the right side of the house. They would each take four bottles with them. Todd would cover the front with the last of the bottles.

Todd told them to be sure the cloth was soaked with gas. Then light it and throw it – quickly. He cautioned them to make sure that the bottle went in a window or against a door and that the bottle broke when it hit. Just as they headed for their respective spots, Todd heard the phone ring. "Move it!" he yelled and they took off.

Jimmy got to the back quickly. He pitched a bottle against the back door and one through the kitchen window. Then he heaved one through a small upstairs window. He looked for another target, but couldn't see one on the house. He spun around and sent the last one into the chicken coop.

Ted and Eddie had similar prospects. Two windows on the ground floor and two upstairs. They threw their bottles and ran for the truck.

For his part, Todd aimed a bottle at the front door and let fly. Another bottle went through an upstairs window and a third through a downstairs window. The last one went through the living room window. Todd heard the other bottles landing. The other three guys were heading his way fast. Todd watched as the house exploded in flame. The effect was mesmerizing. Everyone jumped into the truck and Jimmy took off out of the yard and down the road toward town.

When they got back to town, Jimmy dropped Todd at the theater and took the others to Todd's house to wait for Todd to return. Todd gave them the keys so they could enjoy the contents of the downstairs refrigerator while they were waiting.

Todd went back in the theater and rejoined Jeanie. For some reason she was not in a good humor. Todd just said he couldn't help being sick. He quickly returned her home after the movie and joined the others at his house.

Chapter 16

Escape!

Lisa and Nela had been fast asleep in their upstairs bedroom when the phone rang. Lisa got up and went downstairs to answer it. As soon as she put the phone to her ear she heard, "Get out of the house, now!" That was followed by a click. Lisa was no longer a bit groggy. She rushed upstairs to rouse Nela, just as the first bottle landed. Lisa then ran to get Enela from the nursery and headed for the stairs. She heard a bottle smash through the bedroom window behind her. There was already some fire down below. She yelled back at Nela to try to get out a window while she took the stairs in two leaps. The front door was ablaze so she headed for the back door. The path to the kitchen was clear, but the kitchen was on fire. Before she could even get there, the front of the house exploded in fire. The smoke from the fire was black and noxious and thick. Lisa was reeling from a lack of oxygen. The heat she could compensate for, but not the fire or the lack of breathable air.

Lisa called out for Nela, but heard no response. There had to be a way out, but Lisa was blind and suffocating. She felt the slightest cool breeze off to her left. The kitchen closet! What about the kitchen closet? Lisa's mind just wouldn't work and the flames were getting closer. The closet floor! It was the entry to the storm cellar. Lisa pulled the closet door open and lifted the trap door. She didn't bother to take the ladder, she jumped in feet first, letting the trap door fall shut behind her. She set Enela down on a patch of fungus and went back up the ladder. She called again to Nela. There was still no answer. Nela must have made it out a window. Enela was crying excitedly below her.

Lisa pulled the trap door tightly shut. She dropped back into the cellar and picked up Enela, comforting her. She made her way to the outer door. It was securely bolted. There was just the slightest breeze coming in from the outside, drawn in by the heat of the fire. Lisa did not know what lay outside the door. She could only crouch

95

down, clutch Enela close to her and wait. Somehow, she was confident, Nela would find them.

The closest neighbor to the Brown farm was Betty Foster. She lived only a mile farther down the road. Betty was sleeping soundly at eleven. She did not hear the commotion at the Brown farm. She did not see the flames. When she woke at six the next morning and looked out her bedroom window she could clearly see the smoke still hovering over the Brown farm. Betty wasn't given to panicking, so she quickly dressed and drove over to her neighbor's farm. Then she panicked.

Betty drove home, called the fire department to report the fire and then drove back to the site of the fire. The house had burned completely. Parts of it were still burning; the rest was either blackened or in ashes. The chicken coop had also burned. A few of the goats and chickens were wandering around, some scorched, others just in a daze. Betty searched high and low for some sign of Lisa or Nela. There was no trace of either anywhere outside the house.

The fire truck arrived shortly and started cleaning up the mess. The remaining fires were extinguished. The firemen started combing through the house as far as the still-smoldering embers would permit. They found no traces of human remains. One of the firemen found a few molten pieces of glass. Another found a melted mass of something very heavy. That combined with the multiple combustion points left little doubt that this was a case of arson.

The sheriff was called. When the deputy arrived he had a few questions for Betty. All she could tell them was that the house had been occupied by two women who raised goats and chickens. They kept to themselves. They had no vehicle and, so far as she knew, could not drive. She did remember an incident involving their mailbox, but had no details.

By that time the area around the farmhouse had been so thoroughly disturbed by fire trucks, fire personnel, and deputies that there was no chance of finding any significant clues as to what had happened. The incident was just put down as arson by party or parties unknown. Case closed.

That evening, when it was cool and dark, the storm cellar door slowly opened a crack. At first Lisa just peered out cautiously; then she climbed out. She looked around. All was calm and quiet. She looked at the house and began crying softly. She, too, searched for some sign that Nela had escaped the fire. She could find none. Quietly Lisa gave way to her grief. She returned to the cellar, closed and latched the door and sat in the dark sobbing.

Lisa stayed in the cellar all the next day, tending to Enela and waiting for Nela to come to her. When Nela did not come by nightfall, Lisa knew that she was on her own and that she had to take some action. But what? All of their money had burned with the house, except for the gold. That was now melted into a single mass that was far too heavy to carry. And without the mint marks, it would be almost as impossible to spend. The goats and chickens were gone – probably dead or adopted by Betty.

Lisa considered that she could continue living in the cellar - there was still plenty of fungus and water. But for how long? Sooner or later someone would come to tear down the house and, perhaps, rebuild it for another owner. She couldn't risk being found here then.

She might be able to move to another colony, but she didn't know where the other colonies were located. Besides, each colony was founded by a pair of Elders. If an odd individual showed up it could be awkward.

No, there was just one solution. She had to return to the Butte. And that would be no easy task. At best it would take a few weeks – unless she could find a ride … Lisa thought about sneaking aboard a bus. She was small enough to hide in the back. But she would have to go to a bus terminal to get on the bus. And changing buses could be a problem. There weren't enough trains running to try that mode. Besides, she remembered seeing a train once during the bus ride to Arkansas, and they were not designed for small Elders. Then there was the clothing issue. She had none. How was she going to hide her whiteness from any nearby humans? There was obviously much work to do.

Chapter 17
Lisa Hits the Road

"Well", Lisa decided, "if I'm going home, the important thing is to start." As the sun showed its early morning glow in the east, Lisa again left the cellar to see what she might be able to salvage.

There had been some clothes hanging out to dry the night of the fire. They had been trampled into the ground by the firemen. The dress had disappeared; but she was able to find a swaddling wrap and a carrier that had not been totally destroyed. They were filthy and torn, but they would have to do until she could find a stream.

The barn was the only structure that was still standing. Lisa looked in the barn for anything that might be useful. There were a few empty feed bags. With a little imagination, a pair of scissors and some string, she could envision a clothes and scarf. But she didn't have scissors or string. She also found a water bottle apparently discarded by a firefighter.

She ran back to the house and started rummaging through the debris in the kitchen. Everything had been burned, but you can't burn steel. It took over an hour, but Lisa finally found the remains of a paring knife. She gathered the various items and returned to the cellar to wait for dark.

While she was waiting, Lisa crafted a crude blouse from one feedbag and a skirt from another. A third bag yielded a head scarf and a belt to hold up the skirt. She was also able to create crude foot covers. None of these items would ever rate as high fashion, but they might serve to cover her whiteness, at least at night.

As soon as the sun had set, Lisa donned the blouse and skirt. She filled her bottle from the goats' water trough. She wrapped Enela in the swaddling wrap and put her in the carrier with the water bottle as much fungus as she could manage.

Lisa planned on traveling at night and finding a place to sleep during the day. But which way to go was problematic. Oh, Lisa knew that the butte was west of Arkansas, but should she go straight west or bear to the north, or to the south. She desperately tried to recall the maps the she and Nela had studied when planning this great adventure. But she had not deliberately tried to remember them at the time and now they just would not come into focus. So, her route was going to be somewhat haphazard.

Lisa put the sling over her shoulder and took off across the pasture. The way west consisted of forest, so she felt comfortable and was able to make good time. She soon stumbled upon a small stream. She stopped long enough to wash off her garments and fill the water bottle. Then she set off again, following the stream.

Lisa ran easily all night, steering clear of a couple of small towns and any well-lit areas. As the sun was rising, the stream emptied into a small lake. Lisa found a large leafy tree and created a resting place high in the branches. She ate a little fungus, nursed Enela and settled in for sleep.

The next night Lisa started off again, but the forest gave way to flat land and the towns became more numerous. She was forced to travel more slowly and make many detours to avoid detection. By daylight, she had arrived in the vicinity of Fort Smith. She decided to rest during the day, eating and feeding Enela. She found a small creek where she could again wash the clothes and let them dry on the branches of a tree.

The next night Lisa continued her westerly journey. She was now in open country and had lost the cover of the forest. The best she could do was to avoid well-lit areas. While she avoided most highways as a simple matter of caution, she remembered that the bus to Arkansas primarily passed over large highways. Those highways also carried large trucks and many cars. She guessed that there was such a highway somewhere in the vicinity. She decided to try to find it.

Lisa was following a large river that was taking a devious path – first to the south, then to the north. She knew she needed to cross the river, but could find no place to ford it without completely exposing herself. She thought that she could swim across, but she wasn't too keen on trying to swim with Enela in tow.

Eventually, the river emptied into a large lake. The lake stopped her westerly progress. She would have to cross the river to pass by the lake on the south. The only other option was to go north along the shore of the lake. There were a lot of smaller roads around the lake. Lisa had to be very careful not to be seen by the people traveling on the roads.

Shortly before morning she found the highway she had been looking for. It was obviously a through-road with four lanes, running east and west and divided. From her vantage point on a small hill, Lisa could see on- and off-ramps connecting with smaller side roads. On examining the area, she also discovered a large truck stop on her side of the highway. The truck stop was surrounded by a tall chain link fence. There was a building near the entrance. In front of the building was parking for smaller vehicles. East of the building was a series of fuel pumps. Behind and to the west of the building was parking for the large trucks.

Lisa settled into a secluded area from which she could watch the activity at the truck stop. She didn't feel comfortable sleeping in such an exposed area, but she could eat and feed Enela.

Lisa spent the day watching the trucks coming and going. If she could hitch a ride with one of the west-bound trucks all her worries would be over. She knew this was terribly dangerous. But the truck stop was not in a populated area. If there was trouble, she should be able to get away. After all, she was a lot faster than any human she had seen, even if she were burdened with Enela and her diminishing food. Also on the positive side, if all else failed, she could get across the lake by following the highway.

Chapter 18

Do You Need a Lift?

Shortly after dark, Lisa made her way to the rear of the truck stop. She easily scaled the fence and made her way to a truck that had come from the east. She waited patiently in the shadows by the truck.

When the driver returned to the truck, she approached him and asked for a ride. He took one look at her, and sneered, "Why should I break the rules by giving a ride to a filthy truck-stop whore?" He then pushed Lisa aside, climbed into his truck and left.

Undaunted by her first rejection, Lisa tried again, and again, and again. No one had threatened her with violence, but no one was willing to give her a ride. After several rejections – Lisa had lost count – she just sat down wearily on the step of a truck. She tried to figure out what she should do next, but she couldn't get her brain to function. She just cuddled Enela close to her as her eyes welled with tears.

"Hello, there. Waiting for someone?" The voice startled Lisa out of her reverie. She was so tired she hadn't even heard the man approaching. She almost fell in her urgency to get to her feet. Her headscarf slipped off in the process.

Lisa looked up at the man. He appeared youngish, with short brown hair and a day's growth of beard. He was wearing a plaid shirt, blue jeans and western boots. He wasn't frowning – yet.

"I'm sorry," Lisa began, "I'm just so tired." She scrambled to replace her scarf.

"You running away from home?" he asked softly.

"No, I'm trying to get home." Lisa confessed.

"No money?"

"Not a penny."

"Where you headed?"

"Arizona."

"Wow! You are a long way from home. I wish I could help you, but I 'm not allowed to carry passengers. I take it you haven't had much luck."

"No, no one wants to help us. That's okay. Thanks for not yelling at me." Lisa slowly turned and started to walk off to find another truck.

"Wait a minute," the driver called after her, "Who is 'us'?"

"My baby and I" Lisa replied, hugging the sling enclosing Enela.

"Baby?' the young man asked. "The yelling and pooping variety?" His voice indicated a certain amount of disgust.

"Oh, no!" Lisa exclaimed. "My baby neither yells nor poops."

The young man chuckled quietly at Lisa's proclamation. There was a somewhat awkward moment of silence. Then the driver said, "I'm going through Arizona. But I have a couple of stops to make before I get there. I may be tetched, but I'll give you a ride – if you follow the rules."

Lisa stopped in her tracks and turned back to face the truck driver. "What are the rules?" she asked tentatively.

"No booze, no pot, no drugs, no tobacco and no sex"

"No problem." Lisa couldn't believe it. Was she suddenly beaming?

"Go around and climb in."

As the two settled into their seats, the driver introduced himself, "I'm Rick."

"My name is, Lisa."

"Pretty name."

Lisa threw the food bundle on the floor of the cab and nestled Enela onto her lap. Rick glanced in her direction and took a look at the baby.

"You sure that's not a yelling and pooping baby?"

Lisa was in horror that she might lose this wonderful opportunity. "Enela won't be any bother. She won't utter a sound unless she is in dire distress and there really is no – odor."

"That so? Well, I'll take a chance, but if that baby gets on my nerves, you're both off the truck wherever we are. OK?"

"Fine." Lisa agreed. Maybe now they could safely get some sleep.

The agreement made, Rick threw the truck in gear and he and Lisa and Enela began their journey to Arizona together. As soon as the truck was running smoothly on the highway, Lisa cuddled Enela close to her and fell into a deep sleep.

Rick's first stop was at dawn in Oklahoma City where he would drop his current trailer and take a sleep break. As he approached the transfer facility he directed Lisa to take Enela and all her belongings and get into the sleeper compartment. They were not to make a sound or open the curtain until he told them to come out.

Rick backed his trailer into a service bay where it was disconnected from his tractor. He then drove the tractor over to a separate area of the facility.

"I've got to get some sleep," he told Lisa after he had parked the truck in an isolated spot next to a boundary fence. "If you need to relieve yourself, you can do it between the truck and the fence. No one will see you. The shutters are down, so we will not be disturbed until 5:00 PM, so wake me at 4:30, if I am not up by then." He then swapped places with Lisa.

Lisa had the cab to herself. She ate some fungus and washed it down with a quick gulp of her water. Then she let Enela nurse. Lisa waited as long as she comfortably could. Then she looked around outside the truck. Seeing nothing, she opened the door a crack, slipped out, emptied her bladder and quickly climbed back inside.

Now there was the problem of Enela's swaddling wrap. It was a little more than damp. It needed to be washed. Lisa unwrapped Enela, wrung out the swaddling cloth, soaked it with the remaining water and wrung it out again. It was still damp, but it was unlikely to start stinking. She wiped down Enela and rewrapped her. Then she had nothing to do until 4:30 appeared on the dashboard clock.

Rick was awake and active right on time. He had shaved and changed clothes before he appeared again. Lisa moved into the sleeper as Rick drove back to the main area of the transfer point. He contacted dispatch via radio and got his new bay assignment. On the way, he stopped at a small café to pick up some food.

"Do you want something to eat or drink?" he asked Lisa.

"You forget, I have no money," she answered.

"My treat," Rick suggested.

Lisa was very impressed with Rick. Why couldn't all humans be a nice as he was? That would eliminate all the Elders' problems.

"Could I have a little milk and some water?" she asked.

Rick leaped down from the cab and returned in a few minutes with a sack full of food for him and the items Lisa had requested. Then he backed into the designated bay, hooked up a new trailer, and was back out on the road west.

Lisa remained in the sleeper until they were back on the road again. Lisa did her best to hide her appearance from Rick, but he was too bright a young man to be fooled for long.

They were approaching Amarillo when Rick finally broached the subject. "You must have been through a lot before we met."

"What do you mean?" Lisa was starry skies and not paying much attention.

"I know how some people can get down on you if you look different. I can imagine you've had some problems." The comment was neutral, but it shocked Lisa back to reality. She looked at Rick and suddenly realized that they had become far too chummy for her comfort.

Lisa decided that a direct assault might be the best approach. "You think I 'look different'?"

"No... Well.... Oh, forget it. I was out of order."

"At the rate we're going, we'll be in Arizona soon, and I'll be leaving you. I really do like you Rick and I am very grateful for everything you have done for us, but after we part, perhaps it would be best if we forgot we ever met."

The remainder of their time together was spent quietly. Lisa cuddled Enela and spent most of the time watching the road and listening to Rick on the radio. When Rick and Lisa did occasionally glance at each other they only managed weak smiles.

Rick's cab was loaded with radio equipment. He explained that he had a CB radio for short range road condition reports, a single sideband radio for longer range, and a company radio for talking to dispatchers at the various transfer points. As they passed through Albuquerque, Rick started up a conversation with another driver for his company who was called, 'Joe'. Joe appeared to be a couple of hours behind Rick and was also headed for Arizona.

Lisa had been studying one of Rick's maps. "We'll be going through Holbrook, won't we?"

"Yes, in an hour or so."

"Will you let me off there?"

"Of course, if that's what you want."

It was already dark when Rick stopped just outside of Holbrook. Lisa thanked him profusely for all of his help. She took Enela, her remaining food and a bottle of water and climbed down from the cab of the truck. As Rick drove off she read the name on the side of the trailer. It said, "Trans National Trucking".

Lisa had rested during the trip from Arkansas and she had little but open desert between her and the Butte. She hoisted Enela onto her right hip and the food on her left and set off at a good trot. There would be no rest until she got home, some hundred miles south.

As soon as Lisa left the interstate, the night became dark. There were clouds overhead and the moon was not full. The desert was not well lit at night. Lisa didn't mind, she had grown up on the desert – well, to be perfectly correct, she had grown up inside a butte in the middle of the desert. Her eyes quickly accommodated to the low light level and she could move at ease.

She used the road in the distance as a guide to keep her going in the right direction. She let her mind wander as her running became automatic. Occasionally she would take a sip of water or a nibble of fungus to keep her energy level up.

Soon Lisa left the desert and made her way into the Apache National Forrest. It was cooler in the forest, but she could not move as quickly. Still, she enjoyed the change of scenery. The forest sort of reminded her of the farm in Arkansas.

Then the forest was behind her and she was into the northern Apache reservation. Here she had to be careful of small, dark villages or camps. She carefully crossed a highway. And continued on to the south. She was beginning to tire and she still had to cross the Salt River.

Lisa had already decided to use the highway bridge to cross the river. She approached the bridge with great caution. She again welcomed the dark of night. It would not only hide her from others, but vehicles' headlights would identify them. Lisa waited on the north side of the bridge until she was certain that there were no vehicles in sight in either direction. Then she sprinted across the bridge as fast as she could. Just past the bridge Lisa turned off on Reservation Road.

Reservation Road was a thin strip of asphalt that separated the sacred area of the reservation on the west from the common area to the east. It was originally put in to provide easy access to the 'Old West' town of Wakulla and its casino. No trucks were allowed on the road without specific dispensation from the tribe. At the early morning hour, there would be little to no traffic. Lisa just followed the road south.

Lisa was getting very tired. She had already covered a considerable distance A little more desert Lisa thought and she would be able to see the butte in the distance. She was almost home.

True to her reckoning, about an hour later Lisa could just barely make out the large butte in the distance. That gave Lisa an emotional lift. Only another hour and she would be inside the butte. She kept on doggedly putting one foot in front of the other.

In her exhausted state, she did not hear the approaching truck.

Epilogue

The Elders had carefully noted the history of human activity. Humans, they found to be warlike, ignorant, bigoted and generally despicable creatures. They wanted nothing to do with them. Oh, certainly, there were exceptions. But the vast majority were scary. The Elders couldn't even imagine what these people would do if they discovered that a large group of aliens had been living among them.

The Elders had nothing to offer the humans in trade for good treatment. All of their technical knowledge had been lost when the Elders fled their home world. Several humans had attempted to guide their kind in proper behavior, morals and ethics. None had made any significant impact. Surely, the Elders would have no better success.

Now, the Elder community was faced with a true dilemma. The Butte in which they had been living for one thousand years was too small to comfortably contain all the Elders. The excess had to go somewhere.

The only answer to their problem appeared to be the creation of new colonies which could absorb the overflow from the butte. So it was decided to let certain, well-screened couples emigrate to other locations. There they would establish new colonies and slowly populate them.

Such was the effort that Lisa and Nela attempted. And, like some other couples before them, they failed. They did nothing wrong. They just ran into a buzz-saw of human ignorance and bigotry.

Along the way they made a few good friends, among whom were: Betty, who lived at the farm down the road; Maud, the radical realtor; and, at the end, Rick, the friendly trucker. But these few were insufficient to prevent disaster. Jimmy, who began as a friend, became, as a result of simple peer pressure, a complete traitor.

But our story is not finished. There are some loose ends to tie up.

First, what happened to Nela and Erisa? Lisa was already awake when the Molotov Cocktails started exploding. She yelled for Nela and sent her a sufficiently strong mental jolt to ensure that she would wake to the danger. But Lisa's only thought at the moment was the safety of her daughter. After the fire, Lisa noted that a dress had disappeared from the clothes line. But there was no indication as to what happened to it. Certainly Nela could have grabbed it as she and Erisa fled the fire. Lisa waited in the "grow" room for Nela to come and find her. But Lisa locked the outer doors. It is certainly possible that Nela did return to look for her. Finding the doors locked, she could have knocked and received no answer because Lisa was soundly asleep.

Or, both Nela and Erisa could have perished in the flames. True, no one found any trace of remains in the ashes. But Nela and Erisa were Elders. The Elder digestive system consists of a mouth, esophagus and stomach. The stomach contains a voracious bacteria that can dissolve and absorb any living matter that comes its way, except cellulose. The stomach is protected from the bacteria by a mucous membrane. When the Elder dies, the mucous breaks down and frees the bacteria, which proceeds to dissolve the Elder's body completely. By the time the firemen got into the house, a full day after the fire, any Elder who had been killed by the fumes or the flames would have dissolved.

As to the perpetrators, Todd thought he had it made. No one could tie him to the fire. He had an airtight alibi. Besides, he was the son of Reverend Briggs. But when word of the fire got back to the town, their sympathies suddenly shifted to the two women who had been burned out. Everyone wanted to know how the women were doing and how the fire got started.

The fire inspector had no trouble in determining that the fire was arson; it was intentionally set in several locations at once. He also reported that there were no signs of remains among the ashes. The town was again talking about the women at the farm. What had happened to them? Only this time there were no shouts of 'pervert' or 'lezzie'.

The fire inspector also reported that some pieces of bottle were found with clear fingerprints on them and a partial tire tread that didn't belong to a fire truck or police car.

The police chief was peppered with questions wherever he went. His stock answer was that the farm was not in his jurisdiction. He directed all enquiries to the county sheriff's office. They only said that the case was under investigation. Then, one day, the sheriff received a phone call from a young woman who apparently was crying. She encouraged them to seek their answers from a certain Todd Briggs who had left her sitting in a theater on the night of the fire.

Todd's alibi suddenly unraveled. In a few weeks, he and Eddie and Jimmy and Ted were charged with arson, tried and convicted. There was insufficient evidence to charge Bob with complicity in the crime.

The loss of the farm had no impact on the Elder community. It wasn't the first attempt at colony building that failed, and it would not be the last. It was only where intolerance persisted that the Elders had any problems. Most new colonies actually took root and grew. The humans around these colonies found the Elders to be good neighbors. They also never learned that they were actually aliens.

The last question remaining ... Will Lisa and Enela actually get back to the butte?

== 30 ==

www.ingramcontent.com/pod-product-compliance
Lightning Source LLC
Chambersburg PA
CBHW030643130626
46552CB00002B/986